CLACKAMAS LITERARY REVIEW

2008, Volume XII

Clackamas Community College, Oregon City, Oregon

CLACKAMAS LITERARY REVIEW

Editors

Andy Mingo
Trevor Dodge
Sue Mach

Assistant Editor

Heather Frazier

Editorial Assistants

Holli Hunt
Robert Brown
Kyleen Reba
Andrew Arbow
Greg Stein

Cover Art

Ken Nguyen, "Float Series.1"

The Clackamas Literary Review is published annually at Clackamas Community College. Manuscripts are read from September 1st to January 31st and will not be returned. By submitting your work to CLR, you indicate your consent for us to publish that work in our print journal and on our website. Issues are available at amazon.com for $13.95. Clackamas Literary Review 19600 S Mollala Avenue, Oregon City, Oregon 97045. ISBN 0-9796882-1-3. Distributed by Ingram Periodicals, Inc.

http://www.clackamasliteraryreview.org

CONTENTS

STUDENT PUBLISHING CONTEST

Editors' Note

Dear Friends,

We are humbled and haunted by the authors in this issue, so much so that we could not stop ourselves from sharing them with you. See, we need your assistance to help us get the proper distance and perspective.

But here's the trick of it, and almost certainly the part we probably shouldn't tell you: soon enough you'll find yourself in the exact same predicament, and you'll be calling on others for their assistance.

And in turn, yet others will be called upon.

And yet others beyond those yet others.

1

And on.

And on.

So please don't act surprised when someone taps you on the shoulder and whispers something familiar. We'll promise to do the same.

Cheers,

Andy Mingo
Trevor Dodge
Sue Mach

Bobby Metz's Headache
Harry Johnson

My career is going well. People want to know me. Women are hitting on me. So why am I complaining to my one and only friend? My middle-aged, white friend, Dennis, who, in an embarrassing attempt to retrieve someone else's youth, has given himself the 'street name' of Dizzle. He's the only friend I had before I got famous who's still alive, and he's taken an hour off from his limo driving job to sit across from me in some upper west side, chai tea/internet place, so I can bend his ear about my persistent, pervasive depression. I don't really expect him to get it, and he proves me right by making lame suggestions like, "Hey, you ever tried one of those day spas? They got cute chicks and Jacuzzis and shit." As he yada yadas on about his last massage, an image of my father flashes into my head.

Whenever my Pops heard anybody talking about modern solutions to stress, he always said, 'I must've got off the bus at the wrong stop.' Pops hated to hear anyone complain. He even hated the word stress. His entire generation was never in pain and never asked anyone for help. He worked construction for forty years, never made foreman, and dropped dead on the job. He tried to pass his toughness down to me. When I was little and tripped on the sidewalk, my mother reached down to help me, and he barked, "Don't! You're gonna spoil the kid." He didn't make me tough, he made me mad. He made us all mad. My mother hated the patriarchal system that made him the boss, my father hated her for controlling his sex life, and

I hated them both for making me think about all this crap. All I wanted to do was bury my face in my mother's massive, cushiony breasts where my father and school and every other crummy thing in the borough of Queens went away. I have been chasing that feeling ever since I can remember. High school was torture, but once I left that social disaster behind, I did okay for a short, hairy guy with mediocre looks and *savoir faire* to match. I knew if I could just bury myself in a woman, the world would leave me alone and I would be happy forever. I spent my twenties and thirties lusting from one female body to another, seeking a cure for what ailed me. As my youth receded further into the past, fewer and fewer women were buying my act. I developed headaches and my ankles started to hurt to the point where I had to give up handball. I ate Motrin for the pain and avoided the local pickup games. Doctors couldn't find anything wrong with me. I complained a lot. The people I had called friends fell away one by one. Dennis suggested I take up poker. For once, I took his advice, but after a year and a half and several costly excursions to Atlantic City, I gave that up, too.

The worst part about my downward, backward slide was that the occasional one-nighter no longer distracted me from the anguish of my loneliness. I tried hookers. They were very sweet, which surprised me, and of course the sex was technically superior, but there was no love. I know it sounds stupid to expect love from a whore, but I couldn't help it. I've been looking for true love forever and good sex was as close as I ever came. For the first time in my life, I slipped into a state of self-pity. Deep inside I realized that no amount of paid sex or televised sports or Jack Daniels was ever going to make me feel like a regular person, whatever that is. I was disgusted with myself and I didn't know what to do about it.

It took an accidental fling with crime to turn my fortunes around. I was cajoled into abetting a burglary, and I, the smartest guy on the job by half, was the only one who got caught. Things turned out okay for me, however. I ended up doing a nickel at Attica because I wouldn't rat out my buddy Nitro, rest his soul, and while I was there I taught myself to write. They had a pretty decent library and it didn't take long to figure out that the screws gave special treatment to peaceable inmates who posed no threat to the prison structure. Not to mention the do-gooder philanthropists and bleeding-heart

3

editors who wanted to help rehabilitate us felons, albeit for their own aggrandizement, which was fine with me. While the rest of the jailbirds were diddling their cellmates and writing pornographic love letters to chicks who sent them sexy pictures, I latched on to middle-aged women with a penchant for literature.

I learned fast. I composed violent, brutal poems. I wrote flash fiction in the second person. My grisly, graphic stories glamorized *life on the inside*. Park Avenue broads loved the power of my voice and couldn't wait to promote me. They loved to get their emotional hands dirty a few minutes a month, so long as their marble sinks and soap rosettes were only a limo ride away. Then there was the exceptional, committed Mrs. Markham, who made the trek upstate several times. She looked pretty good sitting across the metal table in the visitor's room with the guard standing right outside the bars listening to everything we said. She wore low- cut silk blouses under Chanel suits and kept crossing and re-crossing her legs the whole time. She gushed and she flirted. She quoted my poems *verbatim* and promised me powerful connections. She was the one who advised me that memoirs were all the rage as she sat there squirming in her seat, gawking at my biceps and hairy chest. Talk about working the system. A blind idiot could have pulled off what I did.

When I was paroled, I didn't have to go looking for a job with a criminal record hanging over my head like the other stiffs, because, thanks to Mrs. Markham, *et al*, I had been published. My first memoir was flying off the shelves. Precious artsy journals were begging me for material. I had a three-book deal at Knopf. *Vanity Fair* wanted to serialize the first five chapters of my next work. I was invited to every A-list event. People were dying to glimpse me in the flesh so they could feel better about the world they wanted to believe in, a world where hardened criminals could become fruitful members of society, a world where the misfortunate could be restored to a useful place by philanthropic matrons, a world where art is more important than true understanding.

When Oprah called, I told my agent to put on the brakes. Don't get me wrong, I love the attention, and my public life was great for sales, but I'm a serious writer and I was spending more time having my picture taken than I was writing. To Dennis, however, my shallow life appeared to be an abundance of pleasure and satisfaction. His simple, immature dreams could be brought to fruition in a snap by my circumstances.

"Jesus, man, you go to openings and shit with celebrities, chicks are hitting on you all the time, and you got money in the bank. What's the fucking problem?"

Dennis is truly a good guy and would definitely come through in a pinch if I ever needed a last-minute limo to JFK, but he's mentally stuck back in Rego Park, and he'll always be leaning on a parking meter as far as I'm concerned. Still, he's my only friend from the old days and therefore, the one person who's truly being honest with me at all times. So, I pick up the check and he's my sounding board, my connection to my roots. He was the only friend who showed up at Pops' funeral, and he didn't bug me or try to make me feel better. I loved him for letting me grieve my own way.

Mom did not cry one drop that day. I guess she loved Pops the way married people did back in the day, but when he died, she was finally free to pursue her decades-long dream—a modern, successful man who couldn't keep his hands off her. Turns out she had been stashing dough in the back of the maple armoire in the foyer and made some secret investments in beach property down in Neponset, which were now worth a fortune. Between that and the old man's life insurance, she was set.

We are definitely a family of transformation, with both my mother and I turning life-long resentments into late-blooming success. First I go from being an accidental convict to a *cause celebre,* then my mom morphs from the bitter housewife into the rich widow, shopping at Bergdorf's and sipping midnight cocktails at the Carlyle. You'd think we'd run into each other in the moneyed part of town, but Mom doesn't want to have anything to do with me. She sees me as just another jerk who got caught, like some stranger in a newspaper story. She doesn't deserve the title of mother. You'd think after what we'd both been through, she'd at least return my calls. Well, she can go fuck herself. I'm not wasting any more energy on her. She'll die soon enough and be out of my hair. That's what happens in families. Hey, I didn't invent this world. I'm just making my way in it.

All this reflective reminiscence takes place behind my sunglasses as I listen to the personal opinions of Dennis/ Dizzle, whose idea of a big thrill is sniffing the back seat of

5

his limo after driving Maria Sharapova over to Teterboro. Yet he's the only person on earth I can trust to give me an honest answer, albeit from a brain with an I.Q. of about 92. I drift back into the present, where I once again attempt to explain the pain of writer's block and listen to Dennis's diversion therapy suggestions.

"Hey, man," he says, leaning forward in his eagerness to get through to me, "Look at the bright side. You could be Nitro. At least you're alive."

I think back on the horrible hit-and-run driver that ended the life of our other friend, my former partner in crime, and I kinda see his point. Kinda.

"That's one way of looking at things, I suppose, but it's not enough."

He stares at me, incredulous.

"What's the matter with you, Bobby? Don't you want to be happy?"

Ouch, man. Finally, he said something that knocked on my door, but I wasn't in the mood to go there. Some other time.

"C'mon man, you know what I mean. It's too simplistic. I can't feel better just because I'm not dead."

Dennis continues to talk and I go in and out of daydreaming again. Thank God for sunglasses. My head is throbbing. This time my mind recalls, as it does so often, the tall, strawberry blond Julie Sykes, the girl with the cushiony breasts that I was crazy about in high school. The girl who looked straight through me because I was a short, dark, hairy guy that didn't play sports. I showed her, didn't I? Now I am a short, dark, hairy bestselling author.

What Julie Sykes probably didn't know, and what Dennis definitely doesn't know, and what no one else will ever know as long as I am alive is what happened on Senior Night at the Roseland Dance Hall in Manhattan when I did about a pound of cocaine. The entire senior class, drunk and stoned and terrified of the empty future most of us faced, were dancing like it was their last night on earth. I kept going back and forth to the men's room, up and down the iron stairs, pissing out those Ballantine Ales, stuffing magic powder up my nostrils, and speaking to no one. I was staring at Julie, the girl I had lusted after for all four years of my outcast high school life, the queen of our class, with an unbelievable body and an angel's face. My eyes followed her like a sniper as she danced with her boyfriend, drinking and laughing with her in-crowd, asshole friends that I hated, her unassuming beauty pulling my gaze to her like gravity.

Every source of light in the huge hall seemed to find her long, pearly-satin, strapless gown with a slit halfway up the skirt. Dazzling beams bounced off her diamond earrings, her blond hair grazed her bare shoulders. Her cleavage glistened from perspiration and the swirling disco ball. In my hyped up yet bleary-eyed state, I sat on the same bar stool and ogled her from a distance between countless beers and trips to the toilet. At one point, I stumbled out of the john and saw the untouchable Miss Julie, weaving up the stairs, wobbling on her high heels, heading for the ladies' room. She didn't even notice me in the doorway of the men's room, where I froze when I spotted her. She had a way of not even seeing people who weren't in her league. I couldn't take my eyes off her naked shoulders and her leg sliding in and out of that slit. When she walked unsteadily past me, I whiffed her famous gardenia perfume that had intoxicated me with resentment for four years.

As she approached the door of the ladies' room, I was already in motion. I grabbed her arms and shoved her further down the hall and around a dark corner, smothering her body with mine, stifling her protests with my thick, angry hand. We were far from the dance floor and in total darkness. I wouldn't have cared where we were. I shoved my hand into that slit and tore at her lace undergarments. I opened her with my knees and forced myself into her as she bit my hand. She never stopped fighting. I kept going at her and going at her, but I couldn't get off. The lights swirled and flashed in the distance, the deafening disco music blasting from a thousand speakers. I bucked and pushed, stifling her screams with my hand, pounding her against the wall, my hips cramping and my legs wobbly. I finally exploded inside her as my body spasmed and I jerked my head back and screamed at the ceiling like a bloodthirsty, insane wolfman. She gave my hand one big chomp and twisted free of my grasp. I reeled backwards, losing my footing as everything around me spun wildly in circles. She ran for the stairs. I caromed off the railing, and lurched toward the men's room, puking before I made it there. I heard her sobbing as I wretched, the sound of her heels clacking down the metal steps. I was on my hands and knees, puking my guts up and probably ten seconds from a heart attack. I don't know how long I knelt there before I found the strength to get to my feet and stumble back downstairs. I never saw her again.

The following morning, as my musketeers tried to recall that night of all nights, Nitro mentioned that Julie Sykes seemed to have disappeared at some point. Dennis said she probably rode off into the sunset with Mr. Most Likely, Steve Lucas, in his Corvette, which everyone knew was purchased by his father's plumbing business. I'd bet money we all had the same image in our heads, of her round, tight ass ensconced in a leather bucket seat, further reminding all us losers what we'd never have.

The smart guy that I think I am should have had a morning after epiphany at that moment, but I didn't. Intelligence, it turns out, has nothing at all to do with emotional or spiritual wisdom. I needed some time, some separation from the world, and, as it happened, several years behind bars to see things more clearly. People say things happen for a reason. I say people make up reasons because it drives them nuts when they don't understand stuff. If something doesn't follow logic they don't want to believe it, they call it a miracle, or an omen, or Murphy's Law. People don't know shit. They called it miraculous when a street corner kid from Queens became a fucking *literati*, but the truth is, anything can happen and it often does. If only they knew.

In the midst of Dennis waning philosophical about women and money, I got an urge. I swiped my credit card at one of the computer stations and Googled the site that can trace anyone anywhere, and one more card swipe later, there she was, Julie Sykes, Ph.D., teaching graduate English at Columbia with the same last name, which could mean anything. I turned down Dennis's offer of a ride, promised him I'd call later, and hopped a cab up Broadway to 116th Street without a plan.

It's amazing how quickly you can find out whatever you want these days. One minute I get the notion to look up a girl I had tried not to think about every day for twenty years, and a half hour later I am standing outside her classroom in Morningside Heights. The first thing I noticed through the beveled glass in the door was that the haunting face of Professor Sykes seemed almost as young looking and elegant as I remembered it from long ago. She was wearing tan corduroy slacks with wide pleats and a tailored, peach colored linen blouse that flattered her figure without drawing attention to it. A soft, coffee brown sweater was draped over her shoulders. Her teal-rimmed glasses hung from a plain, black cord around her neck and balanced themselves directly above her memorable bosom. She stood almost perfectly still as she spoke, her erect posture giving her the look of an old-fashioned school marm or a military officer. I was mesmerized.

As I watched her lecture, I flashed back to looking across the high school cafeteria and recalled feeling almost overcome with desire and envy by the simple sight of Julie Sykes eating lemon meringue pie. Still another flashback remained buried under consciously constructed layers of shame. The throbbing returned on both sides of my head, just above my ears. That's when I noticed the cane leaning in the corner behind the desk; the cane with the pearl T-handle and the bottom third painted red. Then I noticed the glasses hanging around her neck were sunglasses. Now what? She didn't know I was there, and it wasn't incumbent upon me to let her know I was. God would have wanted me to do that but I hadn't listened to Him since my arrest. Then I thought, what the hell, I don't even know why I came up here, so what difference does it make if she's sightless? What if she gets too close to me and suddenly remembers everything? They say blind people's senses become more acute. What the hell. Maybe that's why I'm here. Whatever force propelled me uptown was still there, demanding I see it through. I decided to find out how Julie got to where she is from where I left her.

While I waited, I looked at the walls lined with portraits of old-boy types who personified the history of the English department and I reminisced about the arc of my life; which parts would make good fiction, which might spice up my second memoir and which parts were too dull to be revealed for any purpose. The ache above my ears was getting worse. I had a sudden hunch it might be related to why I was nabbed at the robbery years ago, and, for that matter, why I was creatively blocked today. It's no wonder everyone wants to fabricate memoirs, real life is too fucking unbelievable. Every time somebody tells me something that happened to them, it occurs to me that their story would be rejected out of hand if it was pitched as fiction. Yet thousands of absurd events, impossible coincidences, hideous cruelties, and miracle outcomes occur every day. For example, who would believe that Julie Sykes of Rego Park, Queens, had been raped, lost her sight, earned a Ph.D. and is teaching postgraduate English at Columbia? I was more than curious. I stood there, jittering inside like a charged ion, waiting for a woman I hadn't seen for twenty years whom fate and an impulse had dealt back into my hands.

Never having been to college, I was expecting a bell to ring, so I was jarred out of my self-absorbed reverie when several doors opened and the fresh young faces of the future filed past me. As I made up stories about each one who walked by, taking casual note of some of the finest breasts in The Big Apple, I heard a refined, confidant female voice behind me. "May I help you?" I turned to face Ms. Sykes, who was not wearing her sunglasses, who was not manipulating a cane, but rather was looking directly into my eyes and not recognizing me. She stood tall, her head several inches above mine. She carried a Coach messenger bag over her shoulder, and her face did not divulge a hint of emotion. She was merely offering to help a stranger find his way. She was one of those rare people who seemed to view her circumstances without judgment or irony. I was disarmed. And she wasn't blind. One hurdle out of the way. Why the hell did I come up here?

"Hi. It's me, Bob. Robert. Robert Metz? We went to high school together."

She looked a little closer with a slight squint, like someone trying to pick out a perp from a police lineup. My right eyebrow raised a few millimeters. *Does she remember?* She blinked and spoke. "Oh, uh, sorry. You look just like that fellow on the prison book."

"Yeah, that's me. And I'm also the guy you went to high school with twenty-one years ago. Remember? Bobby? We were in Mrs. Laughlin's English class together?"

She shook her head apologetically. "I'm sorry. That was so long ago."

That nagging urge to reveal more was pushing its way forward in my consciousness, pressing against my skull, but I kept the lid on my emotions, continued to ignore my headache, and waited for her to remember.

"That was my favorite class. All I remember was I sat in the very front row so I could make a good impression on Mrs. Laughlin."

I smiled, covering the lust and shame battling for control of my heart and mind. I recalled how great her ass looked from the back row in those snug, gray skirts that outlined her perfect figure. "I remember now, you sat up front. No wonder you didn't see me."

"I'm sorry. Please don't think me rude."

"No problem." I made a mental note to spend more time with people who felt good about themselves and treated others with decency.

"Ohmygosh! Did you say you *were* that fellow who wrote the prison memoir?"

"Yep. That's me."

"Well, congratulations to you, Robert. Wow. That is not your average best seller, it's a very well-crafted, honest, intelligent piece of writing."

I blushed. My face hadn't colored like that since my only high school girlfriend, Angie (Don't call me Acne) Coluzzo, broke up with me in broad daylight in Taylor's Pool Hall in front of everyone who mattered in my life at the time. That was the closest I ever came to intentionally committing a crime while sober.

"Thanks. It means a lot coming from an English professor." I felt a little confidence returning. Her face changed. She tilted her head and looked me over once more, this time with what felt like respect tinted with curiosity. A flicker of a smile curved the corners of her mouth. I felt emboldened. "Would you like to have a cup of coffee or something?"

She looked at me for a few more seconds, which made me feel the discomfort of the guilty. "Ohmygosh! I am so sorry, but I have to teach another class in..." She shot her arm out of the sleeve of her cashmere sweater and looked at her gold watch. "Two minutes, and it's all the way across campus. We can walk and talk, if you don't mind."

"Sure. Let's go." As she led the way, I snatched a peek at her left hand gripping the strap of her bag. No wedding ring. No jewelry at all. Where does a teacher get the dough to deck herself in cashmere and a Cartier watch? Maybe it was a gift from a rich boyfriend. Maybe it's a knock off from the Nigerians on Sixth Avenue. And what was the deal with the cane back in the classroom? Whatever. There was a lot to learn about Julie Sykes, but for now I was having trouble keeping up with her. So much for walking and talking. She was striding across campus like some kind of show horse. This was one of those people who gets things done. She suddenly stopped and looked at me as if I was someone else completely.

"I have a great idea. My next group is Creative Non-Fiction, and I would love to have them hear it straight from the horse's mouth. What do you say?"

"I… I don't know. I mean, all I did was tell the truth in the book and…it kinda wrote itself, you know what I mean? Besides, I'm not exactly proud of what I did."

"Robert, don't be so modest. The bottom line here is that you're a bestselling author of a literate, emotionally daring memoir, and anything you say has 'street cred' with these kids, you know?"

I figured, given my secret, it was the least I could do. "I suppose. Are you sure?"

"Yes, I'm sure. What have you got to lose? C'mon, it might be fun." She took off, not waiting for my answer.

I realized I was even more attracted (if that's possible) to the grown up version of the snob from high school, the victim from the dark hallway. I glimpsed a future where my luck was changing and I wouldn't need Dennis's retarded input to relieve my pain anymore. My instincts were driving me to seek female companionship to fill the nagging emptiness that lately had been striking me dumb at the keyboard. I walked faster to catch up with her.

She skipped up the steps to her building three at a time, yanked open the door, smiled that Julie smile, and grabbed my hand, guiding me down a hallway to the second door on the right. We entered a classroom filled with a group of young people I would describe as smart-looking, whatever that means, and definitely eclectic – the human equivalent of the sampler platter at Spiro's Greek restaurant in Flushing. I stared empty-eyed at the students, as I was momentarily consumed with the sensation of Julie's hand briefly holding mine in the hallway.

"Good afternoon, everyone." The conversations stopped quickly as the students mumbled greetings to Ms. Sykes while giving me the once over. "We are in for a special treat today. We are going to spend half our time, or longer if he is willing, in a Q and A session with none other than the author of a best-selling example of creative non-fiction, which I believe is currently on the Times' list…"

"Forty-nine weeks." I didn't realize I had spoken. I blushed again.

"For forty-nine weeks. Not bad, huh, class? Well, then, let's get to it. Before we start, let me remind you to couch your criticisms into questions as you would with your classmates in a workshop situation, with an eye toward sharpening your own skills and, of course, with respect." She looked around the room as her instructions sank into the now alert brains. "Ladies and gentlemen, Mr. Robert Metz, author of "Not A Fish." The class applauded. Group behavior is funny, isn't it? People just do things they think they're supposed to do. Julie wasn't finished. "I have a question, Mr. Metz. Would you please tell the class where the title came from?"

The hand of an exceptionally pretty blonde in the front row shot up. "I know!"

Julie was still in charge. "Ms. Carlsson?"

"I read your book almost a year ago, and I totally loved it. I remember that because I wondered what the title had to do with the story. 'Fish' is prison jargon for new prisoners, right?"

It pained me to look at this Carlsson chick. She was the short, dark, hairy guy's wet dream; shoulder length, flaxen hair, perfect teeth, bright, blue-grey eyes, flawless skin that looked slightly tanned even in winter, large breasts and shapely calves, all clad in a tweed skirt, a lime colored cotton sweater, and, get this, Keds!

"You're right. Ms. Carlsson, is it? That is where I got the title. I heard that expression after I'd been inside a few months, after a couple more shipments of 'fish' had arrived behind me. It gave me some perspective on what I was in for, and I had a kind of epiphany – you guys know what that means, right?" I smirked as a titter of laughter rippled across the room. "That day in prison I had what some call 'a moment of clarity.' It was the first time in my life I saw reality for what it was and I made a conscious decision to make it work for me instead of against me. The words 'not a fish' also relate to me feeling unlike the other cons - like a fish out of water, so to speak. Oh, and my publisher thought it was 'catchy.'" More laughter. I loved it.

Julie chimed in, "Does anyone else have a question for Mr. Metz?" Every hand in the room went up. I swear it gave me a boner. Or maybe it was Blondie in the front row. It's hard to tell which was more of a turn on, swarms of anonymous literature worshippers wanting a piece of my mind, or the gleaming, virginal perfection of Miss Norway. Some things never change.

The rest of the class flew by. I answered questions for the entire fifty minutes and then some. These MFA kids were smart. I probably learned a thing or three. There was no class scheduled in that room after us, so half the kids stayed and we kept the Socratic thing cooking until Julie smoothly interceded to close the session. When the last student had shaken my hand and left, hopefully on their way to Barnes & Noble to contribute to my next royalty check, Julie asked me if I still wanted that cup of coffee. "And it's on me. You've done me a huge favor today." If only she knew. I caught myself wondering what kind of panties she might be wearing.

"Actually, I've built up an appetite. How about a late lunch or early dinner? It looks like you're done for the day."

"Very observant, my old friend. Like what you said about seeing reality without emotional lenses clouding your perception. Great point, and beautifully phrased."

"Can we stop talking about writing for while? I'd like to hear about you."

She smiled a humble, you-got-me smile and said, "Of course." She flipped open her cell phone. "Let me just call my daughter. She's coming home on her first holiday from grad school and she'll be expecting me."

My brain froze as though I had been force fed nine Italian ices through my nose. Julie Sykes had a child. In grad school. I couldn't help doing the arithmetic.

She kept walking on ahead as she left the message for her daughter while I stood pinned to the floor. She stopped and turned back toward me, her curves silhouetted by the light from the double doors, her prize-winning smile lighting up the corridor.

"C'mon," she said, "What are you waiting for? Let's eat." I looked at her eager, open expression, and wondered what contorted shape her lovely face would take if she knew what I knew. It makes you wonder what the real value of truth is. My double-sided headache was threatening to engulf my entire skull. My vision was fractured by a kaleidoscope of tiny shards of light caroming inside my eyeballs like shooting stars. Pain stabbed my ankles. Up ahead, Julie looked back at me, tilting her head to one side, as if she had come upon a lost child.

"Are you all right?"

I stood frozen in place, silent, definitely not all right.

The Convention
Lois Parker Edstrom

We know a storm is imminent when the seagulls hold their convention. Hundreds gather, tightly packed, in the middle of an inland field, talking all at once. Have they not heard of courtesy? Protocol? Robert's Rules of Order? One, all fluff and dander with a rude, open mouth and flapping wings, is intent on out-shouting the others. Some are haughty, strutting around on scrawny legs, looking down their long bills at the other gulls that seem like reasonable creatures, but are obviously, in some obtuse way, inferior. As a group, they appear to support individual rights until one gull acquires a fractured clam and then there is a clamorous attempt to redistribute the wealth. They are not able to deflect the storm or turn the tide. They give the impression they find comfort and a sense of safety in being grouped together, talking the same language, even if they don't accomplish anything. I wonder if they are democrats or republicans. They certainly are not associated with The Green Party. These delegates pollute.

Mayonnaise Sandwiches
David Starkey

Pat Imel's mother made them
when she ran out of lunch meat,
which was often. Two slices
of Wonder Bread and a thick
slathering of Best Foods.

Then she would drift back
to the couch in that two-room
shack they rented in someone's
weedy backyard and uncap
another bottle of Safeway Vodka.

We, the rest of his band, waited
patiently while Pat chewed his dinner
and watched their black and white TV,
Mrs. Imel knocking back three
or four water glasses of the stuff.

Finally, Pat would pick up his Fender
Strat—the one thing of value
in all that mess—and play
louder and louder, his mother's
stentorian snoring keeping time.

The Venus of Willendorf: Ottumwa, Iowa
David Starkey

She stands in line at the Dairy Queen,
thick-thighed, knock-kneed,
wide and sagging buttocks,
enormous breasts hanging over
her bulging stomach like two
half-inflated basketballs
resting on a witch's cauldron.

Skin-tight polyester pants,
T-shirt emblazoned with
"Don't Hassel the Hoff":
this is a different kind of primitive,
though the body's the same one
her European ancestors carved
from limestone twenty-one
thousand years ago. They knew
then what her stout farmer
husband and their three
chubby kids know today:
excess of flesh is cause
for celebration in a world
where flesh decays while stone
survives.
        As the five of them
take their plastic trays

of shakes and onion rings
and triple-decker burgers
to a booth, I pay silent homage
to this goddess of Wapello County:
totem, charm, harbinger:
sacred mother of all things.

Dancing With Her
Shelagh Powers

There are still moments when the scent of her makes me worry that she has ruined me for other women. Once, months ago, I watched her dance by herself, her white fingers pinching the fabric of her dress so that it swung lazily around her ankles, and I felt as if I could breathe in her smells from across the crowded dance floor.

She likes to cook me dinner even now, even though I have a life entirely separate from her, even though our reason for knowing each other is gone. When I see her she still holds onto me tight, presses me into her, cradles my face against the softness of her neck. My father left her years ago, the same way he left my mother at the start of my life, but when she holds my face in her hands I know that she sees a son, a person to love even though everyone else is gone. She likes to cook me elaborate meals, but always pretends that she'd been planning to prepare them all along. "I have some extra chicken over here, if you want to help me out," she'll say into the phone, and I can picture her standing in the doorway of the kitchen, a floral apron draped over her narrow hips, the cord of the telephone coiled around those long, pale fingers. I always go, even though she lives on the other side of the city and it sometimes takes me an hour both ways. My girlfriend doesn't understand, thinks it's strange for me to continue to visit with a stepmother who was divorced from my father by the time I was fifteen years old.

"Diana is not your responsibility," my girlfriend will tell me, as if I'm simply playing caretaker. I've been with Kim for three years now, and she's taken to speaking to me in that sharp, confident tone of voice that women only use when they're sure a man isn't going to leave them. "If she's so lonely why doesn't she just remarry? It's not like you're related to her."

I was introduced to Diana for the first time when I was ten years old. My father had spent the years following his split from my mother dating loud women who laughed raucous laughter and had no idea how to talk to me. The woman before Diana had long fingernails that she would rake up and down my father's thighs when we sat at the dinner table, whispering things to him while I watched them wordlessly; another one insisted that I flex my muscles every time she came over to the house. She would wrap her hands around my thin, hairless arm and shriek about how strong I was, then laugh in my father's face as if she'd said something remarkably clever.

Diana loved to dance. My father took her dancing the first time they went out, a shift from the noncommittal movie dates he usually treated women to, and I wonder if maybe he knew she was different right from the start. He brought her home to meet me that first night; I'd been curled up on the couch beside my sleeping babysitter, and my father had twirled Diana into the living room, both of them singing "Summertime" in hushed, laughing voices. Diana was tall and young, her gray eyes watery with giddiness and alcohol, and my father's suit jacket hung from her slender shoulders as if it belonged to her own father, enveloping her like a little girl. That was the night I fell in love with her; there in my living room, with my father laughing and my babysitter snoring gently on the couch, Diana had danced me around and around until our breath heaved and the rug beneath our feet lay crumpled between us. She smelled like coffee and cinnamon and soap, bitterness mixed with an almost childish freshness that hasn't changed in the near fifteen years I've known her. Her hair was pinned back that night, wisps of brown slipping from her hair clips and tickling my feverish cheeks when she reached down to hug me goodbye.

"I think he likes you," my dad told her when he walked her toward the front door. My babysitter woke up as Diana left, and looked down at me, confused, groggy, as I sat smiling on the floor, pulling at a loose thread in the rug Diana and I had slid back and forth across the wood with our wild, dancing feet.

Diana's house now is still filled with memories of the life she shared with me and my father. My school pictures decorate the mantle above her fireplace, different versions of me smiling awkwardly out at her small living room; a wedding photo of her and my father stands on the piano in the corner, tucked behind a stack of her music books and tilted slightly toward the wall, as if incrementally she is removing it from its place in her home. She has a picture of me and Kim in the kitchen, a magnetic frame clinging to the refrigerator door above where she keeps her grocery list. She always asks about Kim, in a voice so innocent and curious that I know she's never realized my feelings for her.

"I'm so glad you found a sweet girl," she'll tell me, even though she's only met Kim twice. Even though Kim is not really sweet.

"I think she's drunk," Kim told me the last time we saw Diana together. It was at a family friend's wedding, the night I watched Diana sway on the dance floor all alone, her shoes kicked off to the side, her eyes pressed shut, her lips parted and smiling.

"She's not drunk," I told Kim, watching the way Diana's stockinged feet slid across the marble floor, her hair hanging in loose waves, swinging in rhythm with the fabric of her dress. "She just loves to dance."

My father always used to talk about how Diana had the body of a dancer; she was still young when they met, her stomach flat and her breasts small and round. She wasn't beautiful, but she had the kind of tight, childless body that older women couldn't compete with, and her pale eyes smiled out from her freckled white skin. Sometimes in restaurants or when we walked around the grocery store, my father would catch men looking at her and whisper, "I think he wants you to dance for him, baby."

"I only dance for you," she'd say, and rock a bony hip up against my father. She had the kind of body that seemed to move slowly, languorously, as if she were constantly pushing her long limbs through a rough current of water.

When I was twelve I saw her naked. We were staying at a hotel in Myrtle Beach, in town for a cousin's wedding. My father got us two adjoining rooms, one for me and one for him and Diana, connected by a shared bathroom. I was excited to have my own space, with an enormous bed and a color television tucked into a heavy wooden armoire in the corner of the room. We spent an entire week there before the wedding, going to the beach everyday and ordering in room service.

"This is quite a life," Diana said one night, stretching out across the kingsize bed she and my father shared. We were in their room watching television, trays of half-eaten food surrounding us. Diana was wearing an oversized t-shirt with the neckline snipped out, so that the shirt slipped off of one shoulder revealing the yellow strap of her bikini. "We should just stay here forever."

My father smiled at her and ran a fingernail over her jutting collarbone. He slipped a finger under the strap of her bathing suit and lay back, his head resting on her sun-browned calf. "Your wish is my command." They laughed and she pressed a finger to his nose, smashing it down the way she always did when she thought he was being cute. He turned to me then, giving my arm a light squeeze. "Time for bed, kiddo," he told me, and began stacking up the room service trays.

I went back to my room and flipped on the television. It was late and all the sitcoms had ended, so I watched a talk show for a while. I started to fall asleep, but pulled my eyes open every time I felt them drop shut; after a while I got up and wandered into the bathroom, a part of me knowing that I should leave my father and Diana alone. I remember pushing their bedroom door open from inside the bathroom, though I don't know what I planned to use as an excuse. I wonder now if I'd been trying to catch a glimpse of something I hadn't realized I wanted. I had always liked to watch Diana, enjoyed the feel of her delicate skin against my cheek when she kissed me goodnight, felt proud when she waited for me outside of school. But it wasn't until I eased open their bedroom door that I realized what it was I was looking for, what my half-sleeping body was edging me toward.

Diana and my father were lying silently on the bed, the light beside them still on and shining harshly down on their naked sleeping bodies. My father was pressed up against Diana, a bare leg thrown over her, her damp hair strewn out over his face. She was lying on her stomach, and from where I stood I could see how the brown of her thighs faded to a translucent white over the rise of her hips. It was as if someone had painted a bikini onto her naked body in stark white paint, sliding a brush over the smooth curves but somehow failing to conceal her. Her breasts were pressed flat against the mattress, and I could make out the blush of her nipple peeking out beneath the rise and fall of her narrow torso.

I don't know how long I stood there. I watched her breathe, felt the tumble of my own knocking heart, breathed in the clean, biting smell of her, stared at my father's thick arm wrapped around her body. I wanted to be him in that moment. I wanted to feel my own bare limbs tangled with hers, and I wanted the scent of her long sweaty hair in my face. I wanted the smell of her skin closer to me, next to me, pressing into my pores.

When her eyes opened, I didn't move, and neither did she. She seemed about to speak, and then thought better of it. So she smiled, and swept a piece of hair behind her ear. She held my gaze until I took a step back, back into the dark of the bathroom, and pulled the door quietly shut. I stared at the line of light that crept through the crack in the door, and after a moment it clicked off. I left the bathroom and climbed into bed, squeezing my eyes shut, the image of her body clearer in my mind than that of my own father's face.

The next day was my cousin's wedding. He married a pretty blond girl, a girl with blue eyes and tanned skin and a ready smile. My father kept making jokes about how I had a crush on her.

"Where's your tongue, kid?" he asked me when I was introduced to her. "Acts like he's never seen a pretty girl before." He gave her a wink and pushed my hair off of my forehead with his broad hand. I shrugged and watched Diana. I liked going to events like this with her, events where we danced.

After the ceremony there was a long reception and my father and cousin got drunk on champagne together. My father made toast after toast, then hooted and whistled as my cousin removed his new wife's garter belt. I stood beside

Diana as my cousin swung the lacy belt around over his head, and when it sailed out over the crowds I reached up and caught it without thinking. Diana laughed and clapped as a group of people gathered around me.

"You have to put it on my maid of honor!" the bride yelled to me. She was tipsy and red-cheeked, and so was the girl that came toward me, giggling and shouting, tipping back a glass of champagne as she presented me with her raised leg. I looked over at my father, who was grinning and whooping wildly.

"Do it!" my cousin called out over the crowd over people. "Give her something to remember!"

The girl lifted her skirts, layers of lavender taffeta that scratched against my hand as I gripped her ankle. I could feel the sharp prick of new hair against the palm of my hand as I slid the belt up over her calf. She laughed and lifted her leg higher, passing her champagne off to someone and grasping my hand in hers. "Don't be shy!" she said, and the crowd grew louder.

I slid the garter up over her knee, my fingers catching in the folds of dimpled skin where her leg bent over my trembling hand. I caught Diana's eye, held her gaze as I had the night before, pictured the browns and whites of her peaceful, sleeping body. I imagined the smoothness of her thighs in the tangle of sheets, her small breasts pushed up against the bed. I inched the belt up further, my eyes on Diana, my hands on Diana, my fingers exploring the whites of her inner thighs, the stretches of skin where the sun hadn't reached.

"Whoa, there!" the maid of honor said to me then, laughing and pushing the belt back down around her knee. "I think we get the picture."

"That's my boy!" my father had come up behind us, put his arm around Diana's waist to watch.

Diana rolled her eyes. "You are *wasted*," she said to him, and put her hands on my shoulders. "So I think it's time for your son and I to have our dance."

She led me out onto the dance floor, the hem of her dress grazing my shoes as I followed closely behind her. She pulled me to her, smiling down at me the way she always did, holding my hand between her fingertips the way she had the first night we danced. But this time we swayed together slowly, our bodies moving in wide circles around the floor, gentle and calculated, the dance no longer wild and thrashing as it had been the night we met. I pressed my hand against the small of her back, feeling her bones tight against the fabric of her dress, fragile beneath my touch. Pressing my face to her neck, I could smell that familiar scent, that inexplicable bitterness blended with something powdery and youthful; dancing in her arms, our bodies clasped tightly together, she smelled at once like a child and a woman, and as she held me close to her like a son, I clung desperately to her like a lover.

Dancer
Avery Slater

The dancer holds, one body in the crowd.
　　　　Figures flock around her: steel and bronze.

　　　　The dancer—and the silk rose of her
knee. Bones interrupt to clasp

　　　　their joining space, prepared to spring
　　　　　　　like poppies opening. When she

　　　　　　just walks there is a kind of swayed
　　　　diagonal of grace in every

limb, her limbs like stems, her stance
　　　　aware of marrow, skin.

　　　　Surrounded. But that swarm becomes
a back-drop, wings for entrance, border

　　　　for a stage whose edges press out
　　　　　　　from her, with her: shadows cast

　　　　　　by each potential path she holds
　　　　and balances, while eyes reside

throughout her heart's held territory—
　　　　breast-bone, ankle, finger-tip,

　　　　the lightening nibs of spine.

Scarred
Sarah Rosenthal

Four months ago was the last time a stranger saw my scars.

A slip on my part, a little bit of carelessness-it happens from time to time, and always the reaction is a little different. People blink quickly and look away; sometimes they gasp and mask it with a cough; or, potentially worst of all, they force their faces into staying blank, but a little twitch or strain gives away their pity, and pity can cut deeper than blades.

I can't speak for other self-injurers, but my scars were never intended for public viewing. I've shown them to friends, loved ones-after extensive thought, upon request, at will-but in general I make every effort to keep them concealed. I'm not as brave as my friend, Sophie, who goes out in skirts without stockings, who refuses to hide her scarred legs "to keep from shocking people's delicate sensibilities."

It isn't so much that I feel the need to protect others from me. Most of the time I feel the need to protect myself from them, from their reactions: the gasp, the sigh, the twitch-because in the split second it takes a pair of eyes to cloud over with disgust, or even sympathy, the years since the first time I cut myself fall away, and the pain that inspired the scars in the first place is rekindled anew.

*

I suppose I can't truthfully call him a stranger because we had seen each other before. He was a cashier at the soup-

and-sandwich franchise a few shops down from the fabric store where I worked, and I had paid him for my lunch on several occasions. Sometimes he would squeeze my hand a little as he gave me my change, and I'd look up to see him smiling before he turned and took another order.

I didn't know his name, and he didn't know mine. We had never exchanged any words outside of "That'll be six-forty" and "Thanks" and occasionally "Have a good one."

During my lunch break that day, I had decided to walk further down the plaza and eat in a café I'd frequented since childhood. Once I was settled at a table and given a menu, I started unwinding the endless lengths of my shaggy scarf from around my neck, seeing the restaurant in flashes between slides of brown fabric. It was too hot out for the scarf, but I didn't care; I'd knitted it myself and its weight around my throat was comfortable and safe.

Only after I'd set the scarf in my lap and sipped my water did I notice the boy sitting at the next table. He was already looking at me, and when our eyes met, he grinned. He was still wearing his work apron, embroidered with the logo of the restaurant franchise. Usually our lunch breaks didn't coincide; maybe he was there only because I was there. The edge of his table was about a foot away from the edge of mine.

"Hey," he said. "How are you?"

We fell into a rhythm of nervous, friendly banter, pausing only when the waitress returned to take our orders. "Are you two together?" she asked. "Would you rather sit at the same table?" I might have imagined that the light dulled in the boy's eyes, disappointed, perhaps, when I said, "Oh, no, thanks. This is fine."

My meal arrived first, a Mediterranean omelet with spinach and feta cheese and black olives. The colors in the omelet clashed, the black against the sunny yellow and pebbly white and rich emerald green, and the boy peered over at my dish with curiosity as I sprinkled salt and pepper on my potatoes.

My chest felt hot inside as I swallowed the first bite of eggs, trying to keep myself from wondering too much about why he seemed so interested in me. "What did you get?" I asked, looking over at the empty space in front of his coffee mug. "You ordered before I did."

"That's true. Just pancakes," he answered, then chuckled sheepishly, looking away. "Maybe waiting will make them taste even better."

*

When I first cut myself, I knew what I was doing. At least, I had a vague sense of what self-injury was supposed to be. Like the rest of my age group, I had been raised on films, books, and television that portrayed the self-injurer as one of three stereotypes: the attention-starved teen carving anguish into her arm; the madman on a cold cell floor, digging furiously into his chest with his fingernails; and the pious martyr opening flows of blood in exchange for sainthood and a place next to Jesus on the cross.

Even as a child, these images had unsettled me in some way I could never quite grasp. A scene from a made-for-TV movie, depicting in grainy quality a girl with black-smeared eyes as she dragged a knife unconvincingly across her wrist, left me vaguely rattled-not so much by the blood, or the idea of deliberate pain, but more by the laughable melodrama associated with the act. It wasn't until my adolescence, when I myself began to self-injure, that I realized why such images had always irritated me. They were lies.

29

The first time I cut myself, I was fourteen. I wasn't a fanatic, and I wasn't hurting myself so that others could see it; I wasn't insane, though sometimes I felt that way.

I cut myself because I was full of emotions I felt I had no other way to express or alleviate. I was angry, sad, afraid, self-loathing, and repressed. By inflicting pain on myself in private when the feelings got to be too much, I was distracting, soothing, and punishing myself all at once.

As time passed I began to realize that, if I felt no particular connection with any stereotype of the self-injurer, then perhaps I fell into an altogether different category. Or perhaps, I thought, that was the problem-perhaps self-injury had no categories at all; perhaps it was simply a shared behavior, unique to each person who surrendered to it, and the only trait common to all self-injurers was invisible, emotional pain.

I was fourteen. I thought that I was a terrible person, and that each of my weaknesses-my awkwardness, my homeliness, my inability to measure up to my own impossible standards-was an individual failure on my part, a sign that I was worse than, smaller than, less than.

The waitress came back, balancing the boy's plate of pancakes on spread fingers. She gave us both a significant smile as she reached down and the plate made a clacking sound on the tabletop in front of the boy's curled, expectant hands. Then she was gone.

"I hope they're worth the wait," I ventured.

"They look pretty damn delicious to me." He picked up the syrup and drizzled it in a circle around the perfect scoop of butter on the center of the top pancake.

The two of us ate in silence, too unfamiliar with one another to bravely forge into conversation through mouthfuls of food. When he ran out of sugar packets for his coffee, I handed over one from my table, and his fingers lingered around mine as if he were giving me back my change.

"Hey," he said, just as I took another bite of potatoes, "what *is* your name?"

*

Of course, I didn't just decide to cut myself one day. It had been coming for a long time, restless, building. I had been growing more and more depressed since I'd hit puberty, and I would not talk to anyone about it.

I wanted desperately to reach out for my father, my mother, my older sister-but part of the reason I was depressed was because they were depressed. There was a long history of emotional instability in my family, particularly on my father's side: a blend of lower-class Jewish Americans and European Holocaust survivors, they passed to my father's generation, and then to mine, not only the depressive genes they'd had before the war, but the pessimism and fear they had acquired from fleeing it.

In the end I chose to keep silent, and never shared anything with anyone. My family seemed so fragile that I couldn't bear to put any more stress on them, and I feared what might happen if, in trusting them, they should let me down. At the same time, I had seen the effects of mental illness on my grandmother, my father, and my older sister, and I feared what would happen if I too turned out to be "crazy." I didn't want to feel too terrified to leave the house, like my grandmother; I didn't want to end up suicidal and institutionalized, as my father had as a young adult; and I didn't want to show the world I was unstable and needy by succumbing to temper tantrums or fits of anxiety, like my sister.

I was fourteen, and I had found the only way I knew to release the howling of my mind without opening my mouth.

Years of using a razor for release left me scars, turning my body into a permanent reflection of my mental state. I couldn't have imagined when those scars first began to form that I would never be able to forget their existence for more than a few minutes at a time, and that they would provoke such a variety of strong reactions in everyone who saw them. But even after I realized the consequences of my actions, even after the scars began to form, it was years before I could bring myself to stop. Somehow, harming myself in the most literal sense seemed like the only thing that could make me feel better. It didn't solve my problems or erase my painful emotions, but it created a focus, a temporary calm between long stretches of chaos, and it was all I had.

*

As I turned, opening my mouth to tell him my name, I saw his eyes wide, unblinking, fixed down towards the floor. He held his fork in mid-air, a dripping mass of pancake speared on its tines, and the expression on his face was so impenetrable, so unfeeling that the words tangled themselves on my tongue.

"My name is..." slipped from my mouth in an inaudible mumble as the boy set down his fork and started gathering his things. Although he seemed to be moving too quickly, like a film set to fast-forward, I found myself rooted to my seat, my hands in my lap. I took the chance to glance down, scanning my own body from head to toe to see what had alarmed him.

That morning as I got dressed for work, I had selected a knee-length skirt, tall socks, and boots. Peering under the table, I saw that the elastic of my right knee sock had slipped down my shin into my boot, leaving bare three or four inches of my calf.

A small stretch of skin, but enough. It was the same as what I see every day when I get dressed, when I shower, when I am brave enough to lie naked next to someone: the same flesh, pale from years without exposure to the sun, and the same pink and white scars, overlapping each other to form a mesh that covers my legs, stomach and ribs. I reached down and jerked the sock back up.

The boy paid at the counter and left, presumably hurrying back to work with a half hour left on his break. I watched his empty seat for a while. I watched as the waitress came and picked up his barely-touched plate of pancakes with a quirked eyebrow, and though she looked over at me for an instant, she said nothing.

I had time left on my break, too, so I stayed in the café and thought.

What was in his mind as he walked out the door? What had he seen in me before that instant-and once he saw my scars, what about that earlier impression was no longer true, or interesting, or worthwhile? Had I transformed before his eyes into a caricature, a distortion? If so, what had I become?

The endless list of possible answers to these questions spun slowly in my mind as I took another sip of coffee. Yes, I was able to put the incident aside, to stay in my seat and take up my fork like nothing had happened-because I have been scarred for over six years, and I've gotten used to those reactions, used to the shock that is so great that it mandates immediate flight from my presence.

That reaction no longer devastates me. I know that it is always a possibility, a risk unique, not to me but to self-injurers, a risk we tend to guard against at every moment.

But it still aches. In fact, it causes me more pain than the wounds ever did, even when I had freshly inflicted them on myself. This reaction is what I fear most, what makes me constantly alert and aware of myself, at all times checking, double-checking. The sight of disgust in the eyes of strangers makes me more ashamed of myself than the scars alone could ever make me feel.

"My name is Sarah," I said to myself, to my omelet-to the black olives and white lumps of feta in their fluffy yellow bed of eggs.

He would never know my name.

A Shadow's Life
Jim Irons

Where was Kafka's mother
the night his father

locked him on the balcony?

Kafka's mother,
a breeder of shadows,

the shadow who bore him.

Kafka lived a shadow's life.

Born of a shadow,
he lived his life

in the shadow of his father.

A shadow has no substance.

That is why
Kafka never had children.

A shadow only loves
other shadows

and craves silence

(a newborn's cry will
shatter the silence).

As far as shadows go,
you can get no larger—

Kafka striding across
the planet—

casting his shadow from
Prague to Amerika.

We call his shadow
"Kafkaesque."

And we live in his
shadow

when we quiver before
our employer

or when our own
father calls on the telephone.

Kafka Said

Jim Irons

"We are the result of God's bad mood,"
as if one day God woke up
out of sorts, and, out of sorts,
created us.

We woke in the Garden,
for even on a bad day
God could not help but create Paradise.

Then a woman led us all astray
though the serpent took all the blame.

35

Kafka's Desk
Jim Irons

Kafka feared two things:
furniture & commitment.

The solidity of a sofa,
the heaviness of a bureau,

these objects are not easily moved

& requires the same commitment as a woman.

Shopping for furniture with Felice
he would have found repugnant,

as if he were being buried alive
by the massiveness of oak.

Poor girl,
knowing that an apartment must have
a "woman's touch"—

a touch that sickened Kafka.

Did they ever shop for a bed together?—

this man who wrote to his fiancée,

"The sight of the double bed,
of sheets that have been laid out,
of nightshirts carefully laid out,

can bring me to the point of retching..."

this man who only wanted to be alone,

sleep alone,
work alone

at his desk,
the only thing he loved.

Scenes from California

Becky Browder

We were headed down Highway 1 singing along with the Irish Tenors when Jane, my friend of less than a week, pulled off the road and said she felt the urge to get out of the car and walk the next two miles. I should chill for thirty minutes then drive to catch up with her.

38

I said she had to be losing her marbles if she thought I was going to sit on the shoulder of that road for thirty minutes, traffic being so heavy plus the treacherous road, at least where we were at the time. I said besides the traffic and the crooked-ass road, some nut might come up and then no telling what would happen to me.

"Nobody's going to bother you. People don't do that out here." Jane—California all the way, laid back no worries hippie type, hair under the arms and on the legs, always smoking her joint—said. Then she said, "Fuck you, I'm going to walk and it's my car. You can either drive down the road to get me when it's time or wait for me to return which will take twice as long. I absolutely have to walk two full miles down the coast, I just know I have to do that," Jane shook her head and shivered for effect. "I feel it." Jane smiled.

I thought about my southern friends, the kind I've known all my life, and they never would have pulled a stunt like this. Their manners wouldn't allow it. If a southern girlfriend had the urge to walk, she would have said, How would you feel if I wanted to get out and walk the next two miles? or Would it bother you if I got out and walked the next two miles? But this is California and this is how the girls out here are. They're a different breed. Self-centered mother-haters for the most part. In all the years I've been here—ten at the end of June— I've met only one who didn't hate her mother. She does my nails and came from Phoenix. But the California-bred girls are all alike. They want peace in the world, everybody to get along and all that good sounding stuff, but if you disagree with them, they'll tell you to go screw yourself just like a New York taxi driver.

Once I took a yoga workshop at Esalen in Big Sur. A place more California than California itself. The people say they're earth people, nature lovers, but the two weeks I was there I noticed a lot of trust fund statements coming through the mail. A peace-love place is how most describe it. Joan Baez and a bunch of hippies started going there back in the day. I was taking a shower getting ready to get in the hot tubs when I noticed a man across from me who had a bullet hole in his right buttock. I couldn't quit looking at that hole. Being from Alabama I had on my swimsuit and when I looked over and saw that extra hole in the man's ass I wanted to lend him my suit even though he would have had no need for the bra part. Covering up his butt was my only concern.

I've never forgotten that image. I still see it when I'm lying in bed some nights wondering just how someone has sex with him. That extra hole in his ass would be a distraction for me. I picture myself caressing him, then one of my fingers slips into that hole and I feel like dying. My libido flies right out the window.

I had no choice but to agree to Jane's terms. Jane could take her walk and I would sit there scared to death a car was going to ram into the back of me. It didn't make sense to drive down the highway and turn around, come back, then drive down again to meet her just to keep moving. I thought about getting out of the car, but there was nothing but cliff on the right side of me and steep mountain with no shoulder on the left. I was steaming mad, asking myself what in the world I was doing with a nutcase from California as a friend. I knew better.

Jane started walking in her pink flip flops. Her hair was disheveled as could be but with the wind coming off the ocean it didn't matter. She turned back for a quick second and smiled, giving me the peace sign. I wanted to shoot her the bird, but

I didn't, at least not high enough that she could see it. A girl like Jane doesn't have sense enough to know when she's in the wrong.

I was sitting there behind the wheel watching her as she faded away and the next thing I knew a big burly guy with a full beard and the smell of a wild animal leaned into my ear and said, "Hey baby, want a little company?"

Then I felt his tongue slip inside my ear.

"Fuck no," I said. "And get your fucking tongue out of my ear!" I'd come to use the word fuck a lot since living in California. Most everyone, no matter their native language, understood it.

"You puny looking little bitch, you ain't got no tits anyway and I'm a tit man. I wouldn't fuck you if you were the last bitch on the planet." Then the burly guy pounded his chest like a gorilla in a zoo as he walked away from me. He turned back, spit on the ground, and screamed, "Fuck you, you skinny ugly whore!"

I'd been called ugly before. Plenty of times. That didn't bother me. My grandmother was the first person to tell me I was ugly. She was the meanest woman I've ever known and I remember when she died how happy I was. I was ten and thought the rest of my life wouldn't be miserable once she was put in the ground. Her name was Sara and that's what we called her.

I remember one time when she was lying in her bed drunk I walked into her bedroom to have a look at her. Instead of going over and staring down at her, I stationed myself in front of her dresser. I could see her in the mirror. She was a mess. She had dried vomit on her chin and she was buck naked except for the nightgown she'd been wearing earlier. It had made its way up around her neck and now looked like a big blue flowered scarf. I stood frozen looking at her in that mirror.

Sara kept raising her head and slinging her arms towards me, like she was throwing something. But there was nothing to throw. And I kept standing there looking at her in that mirror. Then she spoke. "Billie, I pity you." She slurred her speech the way any drunk would. I wanted to ask her why but I was afraid of the answer. She flopped back down on the bed, then raised herself up. The same words came out. Again, I couldn't get the nerve to ask why. The third time she rose

I mustered the courage to respond, "Why, Sara, why do you pity me?"

"Because," Sara said, "because you're so Goddamn ugly!" Sara fell back down on the bed, this time out for the night.

I felt myself trembling as I watched the burly guy get back on his motorcycle and speed off. When he rode past, I saw the sign of the Outlaws on the back of his hog. I almost peed myself from the fear. I'd just blown off an Outlaw. I started the car and pulled onto the highway.

"Stop shaking," I said, "you're going to wreck. He's gone. Outlaw boy is gone."

I was driving down the highway at twenty miles an hour, well under the speed limit, and the line of cars behind me was getting longer by the minute. A few drivers started honking their horns hoping to get me to pull over, but there was no way on God's green earth I was stopping that car. I was going to find Jane, tell her to get her scrawny little ass in the car, and then I was going to take a bus back to Monterey as soon as we hit a town that had a bus station. Then it happened. I rounded a curve and just as I did, I saw Jane being thrown over a cliff by the biker.

The first second I saw them he had her by her throat, like he was choking her. Then over the cliff she went as he stood there watching her. I know it didn't happen but I could have sworn my eyes saw Jane's fingers giving the peace sign on her way down.

In a matter of minutes, the place was crawling with people, including two highway patrolmen on motorcycles. The biker stood on the edge of the cliff yelling that if anyone came near him, he'd jump. People, including the two patrolmen, watched in awe as I walked right up to the biker and told him to go ahead, he'd just killed a friend of mine and it'd suit me fine to see him follow her down to that deep hole. I reached my arms out like I might be about to help him jump when he reached out to me and asked me to help him down from the rock he was standing on, said he was getting dizzy and thought he might fall if he wasn't careful.

Before I could make a move, one of the patrolmen had sneaked up to the side of the biker and was pulling him down from the rock. I couldn't help wondering what I would have done—helped him down from the rock or pushed him over the cliff. But it no longer mattered. The patrolman was handcuffing him.

The other patrolman came over and started asking me questions about Jane—things like her name, address, and next of kin. "I've only known Jane a short time, but I know she's a massage therapist in Monterey. Her mama lives in Fresno, in a trailer park out near the fairgrounds." I looked up to the sky flipping through the files of my brain searching for the name of that little trailer park. "Shady Branches Trailer Park, that's the one." Pleased with my memory, I smiled.

"Do you know her mother's name?" the patrolman asked.

I said, "Her mother's name is Evelyn Merman, but people who know her call her Ethel, after the singer, so I'm not sure how it would be listed in the phone book."

The patrolman took notes on everything I told him which wasn't a lot because I didn't know a lot about Jane.

"This her car?" He pointed to the old mustang convertible that had once been navy blue, but was now more rust and primer.

"Yeah, it is."

"Well, it'll cost the state a lot of money to tow it, then the next of kin will have to pay the state back in order to claim it so if you're a licensed driver I can allow you to take it back if you're interested. I'll need your driver's license and to have you sign this paper saying you're driving the car back to the deceased's residence."

I nodded okay.

"The state will have to perform an autopsy on your friend to find the cause of death," the patrolman said.

I wanted to say that seems like a waste of resources since she just fell off a cliff but I knew that would sound rude and, after all, I was a southern girl, so I passed on it.

Back in the car the Irish Tenors were singing Danny Boy and I started to cry—both for the song and for Jane. I began singing along, seeing myself slinging back Irish whiskey or dark beers as I did. I've always been one to think I'm Irish even though there's no proof of it. At times I talk with an Irish accent amusing myself to no end.

As I headed north, I reminded myself to take out my Irish Tenors CD when I got to Jane's house. I thought about Jane—no fear California. No sense either. At least no common sense. And I thought about peace and love and the guy at Esalen with the extra hole in his ass. I felt glad to be going home.

Riding at Night
three sonnets
David Shattuck

we found ourselves   unfurled like stars

raised from   the river bottoms

our dreams disturbed   leapt from the valley

we rode down   in the lower fields

unsaddled on the horses   amidst the dull groan of

each beast following   the beast ahead

our pale legs   gripping the muscled horses back

your thin arms hold   the only light

clay of starlight   like blinking eyes

so much like old men   warm in their beds

we become ghosts   of our desire

knowing what is true   we know so little

when it is spoken   our story will be

like mist through weeds   easily forgotten

43

Swimming Pool
David Shattuck

An empty swimming pool, collected leaves
settling down in the drain, a small puddle
of rust-colored water. That, too, was ours
before we moved to the newly cut edge
of another town, in some other state;
a little yard of brown and homely grass.
Standing in the shallow end, I listened
to the trees wave us off, the wind rounding
the plaster walls, echoing. This was home.
At least it was for me-swimming often
at dawn, when the world slept cool in its skin.
That day, before we left, I stood beneath
the surface, with bare feet on the plaster,
and floated in the memory of water.

Canvas of Light and Shadow
David Shattuck

It's late day and you are sleeping
in our rented room.
In a dream, you step out of a canvas
as if I've painted you,
walking among the stubbled, fallow rows,
under a stark Midwestern sky.
You are naked because
you said paint me naked
before you fell asleep, drunk on vodka.
In the kitchen green olives
tumble off the counter;
you'll crush them later
when you walk to the fridge.
Still asleep, you'll enter the door
as if looking for another dream-
another canvas of light and shadow.
I tell you, everything is light and shadow.
Just look: outside our window the city
is covered in ash-colored snow.

45

an excerpt from *Tuatha de Diablo*
Dani Clifton

Rush-hour traffic was just getting its claws into the city as I reached the entrance of Tuatha de Diablo and already the pub was packed. Conversation that competed with the loud music and the smells of stale beer and aged scotch greeted me.

Gus was perched on his three-legged throne just inside the front door. Gus is a demon, of the supernatural kind, but you can't hold that against him. Nor should you think of him as the bent-on-world-domination, baby-eating sort either; like anything that wields power in this or any other world, he is neither good nor evil. He simply *is*. Gus chooses to live a low-key life right here in Seattle, running security at the pub. But then again, where else would you seek employment than from a fellow immortal? Still, I keep a mental memo not to get on Gus's bad side, because hey – he's still a demon...every 6-foot 5-inch, pitch-black ounce of him.

"Watch it Luna; the boss is in one foul mood tonight." Gus's voice is low and coarse, as if he's talking around a mouthful of gravel. Or bones. It took me awhile to get used to that when I first met him. *How does one get used to anything in a place like this?*

"Yeah, I know." I answered, "Who do you think put him there?" As an after thought I added, "Sorry about that."

"No worries, no worries."

Gunnar caught my eye as soon as I made my way past the pool tables. To avoid conversation, he turned the stereo up louder and shot me a stern look. I returned the gesture with a facetious smile and pointed to the sign above the door, which read HAPPY HOUR. I set to work before we brought this exchange up to a full-blown pissing match. Moody immortals can be *such* a pain in my mortal ass.

My shift began with slinging Pabst Blue Ribbon to fishermen fresh off their boats who smelled like the catch of the day and pouring shots of more expensive fare to designer men from the high-rise glass forest. One might imagine a lack of coexistence in such close proximity, one social class dueling with another but each held the same intention: to find escape, if only momentarily, at the bottom of a glass. Diablo's clientele wouldn't change significantly until the sun went down, when those who are more comfortable sliding among the shadows come out of hiding. What they're served runs a little more on the macabre side and Gunnar handles those orders himself. There is a special freezer kept downstairs that I don't open. Ever.

After an hour of listening to the grinding songs of Flogging Molly, Gunnar finally changed the music to Pink Floyd and those who were still seeking solace from the day took a collective sigh.

"Luna," he beckoned, in a fresh civil tone which told me he was about to ask for a favor. "I've got a shipment coming in tonight at midnight and Gus will be riding shot-gun with me out back. You'll have to close up shop by yourself."

"No big deal, it'll probably be dead by then." In hindsight, I wish I hadn't chosen those exact words.

"Great." He gave me a chaste peck on the cheek. "I owe you one."

"You owe me many more than one Gunnar." I countered but he'd already moved on to something else and I doubt he'd heard a word I said. Or maybe he had and chose to ignore me.

Gunnar would be the first to admit, however, the truth behind my statement. I've loved the man he is and feared the beast he becomes. Nobody should fear the full moon the way I do. Gunnar once surprised me with a small velvet box, the perfect size to house an engagement ring, which is exactly what I thought it was. However, it wasn't a ring, it was a necklace – but it was even more than that. It was a .45 caliber, pure silver bullet, wrapped in wire as you would wrap a crystal, suspended from a silver chain. I knew that pure silver is the only substance that can kill a shifter. So in essence, in lieu of a ring and a commitment, Gunnar had handed me the ways and means to kill him. Nobody should ever have to ask themselves if they could kill that which they love before it destroyed them.

There's no sense dwelling on a past you can't change or a future you can't control. To distract myself, I set to task taking clean glasses from the dishwasher and putting them up on the rack. I transferred another case of PBR's from the box to the cooler, served the crowd as it swelled and dwindled and made a list of liquors that needed to be restocked on the shelves. All the while, I tried to fight my mind that seemed to want to go down forbidden roads. I pushed away the thoughts but akin to ignoring that irritating tickle at the back of your throat, the more I tried to suppress them, the more they took hold. I never want to contemplate Gunnar's darker side; how he knows people who deal in black-market flesh or what he does when he shifts and takes to the hunt. And I sure as hell don't want to tackle my own inner, dark corners.

The night dragged on. I kept throwing glances at the big clock over the door in hopes that it would read closing time. No such luck. The last customer left a little before eleven o'clock and an eerie and unusual quiet fell around the place, except for the music streaming from the speakers. I swept the floor and wiped down table tops to keep myself busy until I could finally turn off the neon open sign.

At a quarter-to-midnight I watched Gus escort two men upstairs to Gunnar's office. Fifteen minutes later, Gunnar joined them. The meeting didn't take long and soon Gus, Gunnar and their guests – one of whom was in possession of a new brief-case – descended the stairs and all four exited out the back door.

I finally decided to call it an early night. I flipped the switch to cut the lights in the windows and crossed the room to lock the front doors. But just as I reached the entrance the hairs on the back of my neck stood on end as a prickling sensation of violent energy flooded my senses. That's when the front doors crashed open and six men charged in; violent energy embodied. Instinct took over – I ran and dove behind the bar to the 9mm Glock that's stored there.

Adrenaline and reflexes kicked in; the name of the game was to kill or be killed. I jumped up and shot the first man in front of me at point blank. Bits of him sprayed across the counter but nobody would notice that for a while. The second one was almost on me so I shot and dropped him before even taking a breath. The others may or may not have been armed – I didn't take the time to inventory. My bad. The rules of this game were cut and dried and the next three that rushed me dealt themselves losing hands.

The sixth intruder didn't slow up his charge; in fact it seemed to fuel his fire. With a primal scream he leapt over the bar with speed and agility that wasn't completely human. I fired and caught him in the shoulder, but he kept coming. I brought the Glock up for a head shot, but the guy grabbed the barrel and twisted. I looked him in his eyes and pulled the trigger anyway. The bullet tore through his palm and the pungent smell of cauterized flesh was instantaneous. That's when his eyes went vamp.

Oh shit!

I was no match for him at that point. He grabbed me by my neck, lifted me off the floor and slammed the back of my head into the vertical support beam that ran up the wall. That single blow should have killed me. The room took off like a tilt-a-whirl and the floor rushed up to meet me just as a black wolf the size of a pony crashed through the back door. In one leap it took my assailant in the chest and drove him to the floor. I watched Gunnar's wolf rip his throat out just as the world went black.

Stars swam through my awareness as I began to float to the surface of consciousness. My brain throbbed more then could possibly be healthy and I felt the immediate need to throw-up, a reflex I fought with every ounce of determination I possessed.

From the scent of leather and aged wood, I knew I was on the couch upstairs in Gunnar's office. Even though the lights had been dimmed, each attempt to crack open an eyelid resulted in a critical shot of pain that split through my temple, which caused me to silently curse and pray to God to just let me die.

"Luna?"

"Unless you're God, go away." I groaned.

"Luna can you open your eyes?"

"No."

"Can you at least try?"

"Jesus Gunnar-" I tried to sit up to yell at him but moving was the *wrong* thing to do. Pain and bile rose up and I tasted both on the back of my tongue.

Gunnar placed a hand on my forehead and his touch sent bolts of warmth through my skull. Suddenly, the disabling pain receded to a more manageable level. My lids fluttered, then opened and I looked straight into his eyes which were no longer the dark eyes of his Irish heritage, but yellow wolf eyes. The pain and nausea eased with each breath I took and as much as I preferred to feel whole again, I despised that it was Gunnar who could mend me like this. One touch from him and I was restored; a mixture of his otherworldliness and our being soul twins. God had a wicked sense of humor.

"What happened?" He asked.

Gingerly I sat up and once I had mentally collected all the details, I retold the event.

"The first five were amateurs but that last bastard had a touch of bad blood in him. He slammed my head like it was a coconut. That's when you – er, your wolf – came in and relieved him of that part between his chin and chest."

50 I shifted my gaze once again to Gunnar's eyes and noticed they had returned to their human brown.

"For what it's worth Luna, I'm sorry."

"Sorry?"

Gunnar made a noise that I interpreted as *'well, everything really. Sorry I'm who I am, sorry I can't be human, sorry I make your life miserable, sorry for all I've put you through.* His apology list would go on and on.

"I'm sorry you had to deal with tonight. Sorry you had to witness my Wolf at his worst."

"Well, you can't change who you are, remember?"

"If I could, I would."

"No you wouldn't."

"Luna – please." He let go a heavy sigh. "How are you feeling now?"

I put my hand up to my head and winced when it came in contact with the lump that had sprouted there. I was pleasantly surprised that the spot wasn't sticky with blood and none showed on my fingers when I pulled them away. "It still hurts like a son-of-a-bitch, but I think I'll live."

"You're going to have one hell of a lump and a headache but I don't think you're damaged for good."

"Great. I just want to get home and crawl into bed – *alone* – and forget this day happened."

"I don't think that's a good idea."

"Which part, the going home or the sleeping alone?"

A smile crept across his mouth that lit his eyes up and I silently admonished my heart for skipping a beat. Damn it, I fall for that look every time.

"Babe, between the two of us, we just wiped out someone's entire hit squad. And when their boys don't come home, they're gonna come looking."

"Where's Gus?"

"Disposing of the last body."

"How?"

"Do you really want to know?"

He had a point. "What about cops and what about your meeting and the shipment?"

Gunnar let go another long sigh. "Nobody hears gunshots come through these walls, consequently no cops. The shipment is out back or at least I presume it is. Two guys, I'm assuming they were part of the team that rushed you, jumped us back in the alley. Either way, they killed the two money men. Now all four of them are dead and I've got the shipment *and* the money. But let's handle one emergency at a time."

"Eight? Someone sent an eight person squad? Who sends that kind of muscle?"

"That's what doesn't make sense. It couldn't have been The Jesuit; he's the one who turned me on to this new supplier because *he's* retiring."

"So what else do you have your paws in?"

"Nothing to warrant this kind of fight." He didn't deny he was into other things, which was a bit unsettling, though again, you get used to things around here.

"Jesus Gunnar; it's good to know I'm not the only person you royally piss off."

Just then Gus walked back into the room. "It's all clear boss. The shipment is downstairs on ice and the place is locked down." He looked at me as if noticing for the first time that I was in the room. "How are you feeling Luna?"

"Peachy Gus thanks for asking." I tried not to let sarcasm taint my response; I don't think I was too successful.

Gunnar spoke up, "We need to get going Luna. We've stayed here too long after what just went down but I didn't want to move you until you came back from la-la land."

"Help me stand up." He lent me a hand and I became momentarily vertical. The room began a slow spin but Gunnar's touch ran interference and steadied me once again. We took our time with the stairs, my strength and equilibrium returned with each step. Gunnar's truck was parked at the curb just outside the front doors and he helped me in. By the time he got behind the wheel and shut his door, I was feeling nearly normal again.

"Where are we going?" I inquired.

"To the safe house."

"Safe house? You never told me you had a safe house!"

"If I'd told you, it wouldn't be a safe house now would it?"

Gus passed a duffle bag through my open window which I knew would be weapons.

"Everything you requested is inside, plus some extra ammo and the silver." Gus said. He handed me the same Glock I'd just used earlier. "Here you go Luna, I thought since you seem to have bonded with this one tonight..."

"Yeah, thanks." I took the weapon and slipped the clip. Gus had taken the time to reload, chamber a bullet and set the safety. Demons can be so thoughtful.

"Thanks Gus." Gunnar replied "Will you be along shortly?"

"In a bit; I have a few feelers to put out on the streets first to see if anyone wants to talk and live to see another sunset."

"Good, see you later then."

Gus gave us a short, militant-style salute as we pulled away from the curb. We drove through the sleeping city in silence as I wondered what the hell I'd gotten myself into tonight. That's when the thought struck me: I should have been more afraid than I was which made me question my sanity. And I should probably feel some remorse, some guilt – something – anything because I'd just killed five men. But nothing surfaced, not even the attempt to justify what I'd done with 'so the world was short a few bad guys', which makes me question my conscience.

What I didn't know then, as I watched the urban landscape pass by my window, was that the following days would make those men look like altar boys and that evening look like a Sunday afternoon picnic.

Anne Lesley Selcer

Wistloh spider cadence and brain
(each word edges off a turning, tissue paper page).
Windsloth
look, it's larvae.
And we're driving
through the humid day
the TV's tuned to 1978;
terrycloth.
I ran into Jeremy,
this is what I told him.

53

An Enclosing

Anne Lesley Selcer

To want
to whittle
to listen
we, unfolding periodically
but on the longterm
folding
this is aging, it is what it seems.
A house,
a yellow light in the windows,
it's temporary;
it unfolds in perpetuity.
To hold
to doubt
it, swinging in the trees,
a treehouse
ruched and scattering, crumpling
and green
to be
to seem
to grow
to be growing.

Anne Lesley Selcer

This is not desire nor fulfillment but the movement in between.
It looks like a slow motion running slide into a slick of yellow
acrylic, then two bare feet are received into mouths of sun.

55

Dream of Drew's Suicide
St. Francis Hotel, Portland 1998

Anne Lesley Selcer

At the window of the old hotel he thought about the real life of childhood before time is sliced up into neat pieces (he imagines muscular, wild children, the needs of the mouth and the toilet) and a stream of piss ran warmly down his leg his eyes swelled† as Drew bent at the knee and jumped or let go through the window frame over the guardrail out the hotel window into the winter weather of the day.

56

† and you could hear the wooden deck
of the old boat creaking

Crepe de Chine
Diane Comer

The clothing I love is from the past, not my past, my mother's past—the fitted, flattering, immensely feminine and powerful clothes made in the decades before I was born. I was the last of the baby boomers, and the last of my mother's three children. I forget when my mother stopped being stylish, because she was always stylish when I was a child. I remember her going out for the evening, high heels clicking, her clothing swishing and rustling with crisp mystery, her signature scent, Crepe de Chine, wafting behind her. I don't remember her kissing me goodbye before she left us with the babysitter, but I do remember rubbing my cheek against her mink stole and thinking, this is the most beautiful woman I know, and she's my mother.

Years later when I was an adolescent, the beautiful evening clothes my mother once wore were relegated to the edge of her closet, and then to a closet of clothing no one wore and yet no one parted with in the attic. A strapless evening dress in peacock brocade, a black silk faille cocktail dress, an electric blue wool dress with matching satin trim, and, my favorite, a green and fawn striped silk summer dress with a net underskirt. I had played reverent dress-up in these clothes for years, and then, when I was old enough to want to wear her dresses in public, they had vanished from my mother's closet. I was bereft. These were the most beautiful clothes I knew, my exact size, and they were hers, fragrant with the perfume of all the evenings she bewitched a circle of men with her swift intelligence and amused detachment. She was a woman few women liked. She was too smart, too sexy, too snobbish, but the women who were her friends were even more glamorous than she was—and more vulnerable. My mother was the confidante of women who broke hearts and had affairs, while she herself remained faithful.

When I asked her where all her dresses had gone, she shrugged, saying, "I gave them away." Away to the Salvation Army or Goodwill or the Officer's Wives Thrift Shop, and who bought them, her lovely dresses? Now I haunt thrift shops in the hope I will find clothing from a past I didn't inhabit, nor do I wish to inhabit, only to wear. And I have found such clothes. Beautifully beaded black evening dresses from the 40s, wonderfully preserved cotton summer dresses from the 50s, a black velvet opera cloak from even farther back, impeccably tailored jackets, hats made from velvet, velour, fur. When the clothing is too big, I have my dressmaker size it down for me. When I feel worried that I've brought her yet another garment salvaged from who knows whose past, she laughs and says, "I love these clothes, I love seeing how they were made." Every time she opens up a garment from the past she learns how the sleeve was set, the fabric cut, the darts put in, and so the knowledge is not lost. She tailors the clothes to me while my hungry self keeps looking for a dress long gone from my mother's closet.

I remember my mother's dresses more vividly than any clothing I wore as a child. My longing for her lost dresses haunts me decades later, and I wonder what made my mother purge her closet all those years ago. Perhaps the clothes seemed outdated, however beautiful and fragrant from her festive past. Or she tired of them, the way we all tire of our clothes. Or perhaps she needed to shed the past, a past she could no longer inhabit (or fit in), and was reluctant to wear. When I asked my mother and she merely shrugged, saying, "I never thought you'd want these things." This from a woman who saved every last pair of shoes she ever bought, whose closet was a library of leather from three decades, nevermind her foot is a size larger than it once was. Clearly the dresses cried out to be given away, or rather, my mother's heart thought they did.

Now, when I pass the aisles in thrift stores laden with bins of beaters from defunct electric mixers, mismatched crockery, table linens with stubborn stains, abandoned yarn from abandoned knitting projects, I'm looking for only one thing, clothing from a time not my own. I could say I love vintage clothes and leave it at that, but I know it goes deeper, a need to clothe myself in a time now gone, but which has shaped me, even as it has shaped my mother. A friend once told me we are drawn to the clothing a generation older than ourselves. When I slip a dress from the 50s over my head and shimmy it down my hips, am I my mother, or myself, or myself as my mother? What mask is this? For what is clothing but a masquerade of the most potent and ordinary kind? When we dress we're saying this is how we wish to appear. Even our most casual clothing reveals us to others. When I choose to wear clothing from my mother's past, I wonder who I am revealing or concealing and why.

I could be indulging my slender wallet and dysfunctional self buying old clothes in tatty stores across town, as though I could repair my mother's life by wearing clothes she might have worn. But I do not believe this. What I am recovering is myself, my feminine self, through a reclamation of clothing from a time when femininity was celebrated. However 59 limited those times might have been for women, at least the clothing was lovely. I learned to be a woman from my mother, even when later she became sexless in her dress, wearing sweatshirts and jeans to hide weight, bloat, and age. I remember her beautiful even if she does not. And I want to keep remembering her beautiful. Small wonder I wear vintage clothing out in the world of signs and symbols, costumes and drama, while whatever we suffer in our daily and unseen world, as mother or daughter, has long since been relegated to the ragbag or crept into our behavior. Put on a dress from the past and it's as though I was never born in my time, to my mother. I am her before the fall, before she began drinking, before the disappointment of our lives set in and dressed us down. I have passed over everything that happened, rewound the years, cast myself in the starring role, put on her clothing, and stepped out onto the stage. Started over in the present. Which is what daughters have been doing with their mother's script ever since the play began.

Student Publishing Contest

This section of CLR represents the best fiction, poetry, and nonfiction from the talented writers attending Clackamas Community College. In 2007 CLR became primarily a student-run literary journal, in that the day to day operations, layout, and much of the editing had been placed in the hands of future editors and publishers.

In 2008 we wanted to expand the role of CLR by publishing aspiring authors, giving them their first published work in what will hopefully be long and prosperous careers as writers. Again we are pleased by the talent represented in this section of CLR, and take pride in our creative writing program at CCC, which we like to believe helped encourage such creativity. We'd like to thank students and faculty alike for making our publication that much more meaningful.

--eds.

Shiseido Red
Holli Hunt

Disappointment killed my appetite the moment I opened the front door and was stiff-armed by the spicy sweet smell of General Tso's Chicken from Happy Family Restaurant down the street. Takeout always meant Macy had to go back into the office that evening.

She sat at the kitchen table, a cardboard carton of chow mien in one thin hand, chopsticks in the other. The tabletop was tiled with yellow legal pads, all filled with her careful blue script. The calluses of my palm snagged on the silky fabric of her blazer as I leaned in for a kiss. With her mouth full of food she turned her head at the last moment and gave me her cheek.

"You're home early." she mumbled around a bite of noodles.

"Good thing too, or I might not have seen you at all tonight." I rummaged in the drawer for a fork. Chopsticks had never been my thing.

"Meeting tonight?" I asked eventually, after choking down a half-carton of fiery deep-fried chicken. She nodded absently and turned a page, absorbed in the nuances of her latest client. A few more halfhearted attempts at conversation died ignoble deaths and I was left to finish my meal in silence. Macy was never one for talking while she was working.

The scrap of paper in my chest pocket rustled softly with each motion, a quiet but insistent reminder of my shame. I had no idea how to begin this conversation.

"Macy, before you go...something happened today." I pulled the crumpled pink square from my pocket and began folding and unfolding it compulsively, fidgeting like a grade-schooler with a bad report card.

Macy scraped the last few stragglers from her box and sighed before she tossed the carton into the empty sack and began collecting her notes. "Can't this wait, Dean? I'm going to be late as it is." She headed straight for the bathroom without waiting for my answer.

"Yeah, sure. Later, we can talk." I growled to the empty room as I cleared the takeout carnage. "Wouldn't want you to be late. Just don't be surprised when I don't go to work tomorrow."

"What was that?" she asked when she swept into the kitchen minutes later, makeup and hair refreshed, collecting her briefcase and purse.

Nothing. Go to your meeting with all the other stuffed shirts, drinking dirty martinis and throwing around money like it was burning holes in their pockets. I'll be sure to have the house clean when you come home, dear.

That's what I wanted to say. Instead I dropped a quick kiss on her lips and gave her a halfassed smile.

"Dammit Dean!" Annoyance sharpened the movements of her hands as she fumbled deep in the bowels of her purse, emerging with a compact and a tube of lipstick, intent on repairing the damage I had caused. I watched the careful reapplication with a growing sense of alarm. She wasn't using just any lipstick. I recognized the distinctive tube, the same brand and scarlet shade I had bought for her faithfully every Christmas as a silly stocking stuffer because she had worn it on our first date. The one she claimed to save for the few occasions I took her out. She called it her Joan Crawford color.

All the quicksilver pieces of my ugly suspicions melded into a repulsive what-if. The recent promotions, the late night meetings, the lipstick.

Thinking before acting had never been my thing.

Sometimes when I wake up alone at night, I dredge this moment up. A little salt in the wound, a little self-flagellation. In my memory, the scene plays out in still life. Like a flipbook missing most of its pages, a gallery hall series of photographs. One brief glimpse after another, strung together into a gruesome rosary of violence.

My hand fisting at my side.

The blur of motion.

The wet clay sound of flesh on flesh.

The harsh clatter of a wooden chair skittering along linoleum.

Macy in a boneless pile at my feet, a ragdoll tangle of limbs and clothing.

I stood over her, my trembling fist a red smear of lipstick and blood, fighting back nausea. The black rose of a bruise was already blooming on her cheek, blood and saliva and Shiseido Red mingling on her split lip. Her perfect chignon had come loose, and hair hung down her back like a limp animal as she struggled to stand.

I wanted her to rise, towering in her righteous fury. To yell, scream, shout, howl at me for being a jealous fool, for jumping to conclusions. I would have fallen to my knees and begged for her forgiveness if only she had said something. An admission of guilt, or a few tears shed. If I saw shame, or anything other than cold impassionate resignation in the grim expression she wore. I stared down at the woman I woke up next to, who liked her eggs scrambled and her jokes dirty and her movies loud, and found a stranger staring back.

A Prayer in the Redwoods
Kate Rose Bast

(a response to Sylvia Plath and her poem "Daddy")

I would exhume, I would exhume
The beaten heart of you,
And bring you soft to snuffle
down, down, forever down to
this blackened lair,
a redwood cave
a battering storm cleft in two,
And opened wide a wizened
womb to buoy away
your brute, brute
ach, du.

Rest your martyred poet's eye
upon the risen mist and rot to bliss.
Oh blessed view, this
poplar shore and
rain green grass
the water runs clear through.
I would close your
blistered eyes,
still,
in blue, in blue, in this aching blue.

Seasonal
Kate Rose Bast

I will remember this fall puddle,
rusting leaves, pink shards of
some birthday balloon,
your brownstone in the water
unwavering like glass,
your oaken door
rooted in silence.

I will remember the stillness
of your pepper breath
that Jamaican July,
the blessing of your fingers
on my bikini lines
and peeling skin,
the leap of my lonely womb, and
the truffle mole on my low belly
your tongue
made real.

I will remember your sister's
baby in her arms,
small hand loose and
dangerous in the air
reaching for you, for you,
your eyes floating ice and you said,
no, I don't think so.

I will remember the first frost,
my Vicodan stumble down 41st,
red boots too high for this
rude womb occasion,
alone, pausing,
the rack of ribs aging
in Mr. Caglioni's window,
organs gone,
spotlight off.

How can I remember I was
some body with you,

these pale uterine scars
my fiction of you.

66

Something Slipped
Carl Graham

Most of the time life is like a machine. It is like a vast complex mechanism of gears and cogs meshing together, wheels within wheels, grinding and pulling together to some unknown purpose. Perhaps to move the hand of some unseen clock or to play a note within some grand music box, it does not matter until something goes wrong. Something slips and the clock misses a beat or from deep within the box a discordant note is struck. It is only during these moments of slippage that we become aware of the machine at all, of how truly fragile it is and how really insignificant our parts are within it. Something slips and things get scary.

You're driving down a highway and you unexpectedly hit a traffic jam. The cars around you crawl as you fume behind the wheel. Suddenly you see the reason as you pass the wreckage, the fire trucks and the body being loaded into the ambulance. Something has slipped very badly for someone; life will be forever altered and changed for them and their loved ones. This day will be forever known as the Day of the Accident, the Day When So Much Changed. Five miles later you will have completely forgotten about the incident.

Slippage surrounds us. Unless we are directly involved we either don't notice it or soon dismiss it from our memories. The reason that slippage is so uncomfortable to confront in the lives of others is because it opens the possibilities of bad things happening in our own lives, that somehow we are not personally exempt from tragedy. We are reminded that virtue, privilege and luck are ultimately no protection against our own slipping, that we are at all times only a breath away from disaster ourselves. It is only this self delusion and denial that allows us to continue driving from inside our own cars as we pass these tragic accidents and not immediately pull over and flee from the vehicles that could kill us at any given moment. It is only this false assurance of safety that allows us to get into our cars in the first place.

It is from within these moments of trauma, either happening directly to us or observed that we enter the realm of slippage. A place of heightened awareness and a slowing down of time; memories of this domain can either be crystal clear or blurred by shock and by time, but they become forever part of us. Slippage can occur on a personal level or it can affect an entire nation if the events are large enough or suitably shocking. For those who are old enough to feel the slip when John F Kennedy and Martin Luther King were shot and the generation after who felt the world reel about them when the Challenger exploded and the planes smashed into the World Trade Center: all can vividly recall the sense of reality warping for them as their worlds were forever altered. The classic question that is always asked in such cases is "Where were you when you heard the news?" could be rephrased as "Where were you when your fundamental faith in a just and well organized universe was being shattered by events outside of your control?" or more simply "Where were you when the world slipped?"

Sometimes the whole world doesn't slide off its axis in a dramatic fashion. Sometimes it just slips a little around the edges, disturbing us when we least expect it. Reality doesn't get totally bent out of perspective; it just has a tiny bit of its wrapper peeled back, revealing the chaos swirling underneath. Sometimes we are just caught up as collateral damage even though we ourselves were not the intended target.

During the summer of 1972 I was 11 going on 12 years old. I was visiting relatives in Tacoma, Washington that summer and was on my first solo mission with public transportation. My cousins had taught me how to ride the city buses and my aunt had given me permission to ride on them for the first time alone, in order to test my new found skills. I had a ball as I rode about town, transferring from one bus to the next as I concentrated on route numbers and bus stops to prevent the humiliation of getting lost and having to phone my aunt to rescue me. On the way back I was waiting to transfer to the last bus that would take me back to my aunt's house, when suddenly something slipped.

Five of us were standing at that bus stop on that bright summer day, a middle-aged man, an old man, two women and myself. We were all standing quietly, focused on our own business except the old man. He was about six feet, with grey drab features dressed in grey drab clothing. On any other day he would have been invisible but not now, he was crying. I didn't notice at first because I was so busy checking and rechecking the number on the bus stop with my schedule and making sure that this was positively the right bus to get on when I finally heard the grey man sob. I've never heard that sound from an adult before and as I looked at him for the first time he suddenly pointed across the street and announced in a loud yet wavering voice, "I just came from that building.... the doctor says that I have cancer....he told me I'm going to die." No one answered him. The middle-aged man and the two women backed away from the grey man. I couldn't move; I stood frozen in shock. "I'm going to die!" the old man almost shouted. I looked to the other adults for help but none was being offered as they all were being very careful not to meet anyone's eyes. The tall man stood silent now, no longer making proclamations as sobs wracked his body.

Time stood still then, so I will be forever unable to calculate how long I just stood there before I broke that terrible silence. I took a single step toward the old man and told him I was sorry. I couldn't think of anything else to say as he regarded me with empty faded eyes, so I told him again that I was sorry. He began to talk to me in a small lost voice, telling me that he was all alone, everyone else was gone. I kept telling him that I was sorry, that I would pray for him. The nightmare finally ended when the bus arrived and I rushed on and lost sight of him for all time, feeling both terrified and ashamed for not knowing the right words to say.

More than thirty years later I still don't know the right words.

Most of us seem to be cowards in the face of slippage. It took all the courage that I had to look into pale faded eyes and tell an old man that I was sorry. If you want to see what slippage really looks like, go to your nearest hospital and visit the oncology unit. See what naked terror looks like, not in the patients but in the eyes of the loved ones who stand vigil over their beds. See what it is like to have everything you know change for all time and feel the earth slide from under your feet. Tell me then the right words to say. I sat next to each of my parents in turn as they died of cancer ten years apart from each other. Felt the world slide both times and came away no wiser. I still don't know the right words to say.

The Budapest Special

Josh Ahrens

The train is cutting through the Bulgarian night, tracks moving underneath beating a rhythm through the floors. From one end, the station in Sofia shrinks out of sight, and on the other, the headlight throws a long beam ahead. Minutes before, I felt for the first time a sensation that would become like a bookmark to me in the coming weeks: that first hard tug of the engine as it takes the slack from between the cars, knocks me off balance, and sets the scene outside in a sideways scroll.

I am standing in the hall outside the cabins, at the window watching small towns, square homes all warmly lit, with our headlight revealing steel skeletons of industry. The sky is purple, with the amber glow of city light outlining black shadows of mountains and chimneys. The air tonight is balmy and thick, and many others have come to the windows to cool off. My journey north, along the rails of eastern Europe is beginning tonight.

Squinting at my ticket for my seat assignment, I make my way to the cabin, and open the door to five of six seats occupied by huge, sweating, smoking, laughing men and one place open in the middle, where I politely as possible shoehorn my way in. Welcome home for the next 12 hours. They're all staring at me. My thin frame, enormous modern backpack, Levi's, and Chuck Taylors must look ridiculous to these guys in their plain t-shirts and shorts. They are constantly ribbing one another, taking long swigs of beer, exploding into laughter, belching, stomping on the floor and slapping their knees. These guys are great. They are still taking turns staring at me with interest and probably amusement, and I am clearly the sore thumb in a group who must all be family, with the same round faces and toothy smiles. Having no language in common, I laugh when they laugh, and let out a few good belches, which wins me some beer and chips. One asks me where I am from.

"The United States". Confused looks. "America".

"Ohh!"

And another confused look, although by now I know this one.

"Why are you here?"

"I don't know yet."

I learn later that ticketed seating assignments are meaningless and most people just sit wherever looks comfortable, which I guess partly explains why my presence in their cabin must have seemed so hilarious. After midnight, the snoring began, and I found a different cabin with two elderly ladies speaking in quiet conversation with one another. I settled in and fell asleep, watching the streetlights and the occasional car pass by the window, not knowing what I was doing in eastern Europe, besides existing.

The night makes everything different. Wonderful, and sometimes unbearable, it brings out all of the thoughts, feelings, joys, and sorrows that are so easy to ignore during the day. Away from the noise and brightness and color, my imagination, my soul, begin to come alive. Fragments of songs I've made up, thoughts, old memories happy and painful are all coming loose, and moving in and out of my consciousness in weak signals.

I wonder about my family back home, and what they are doing and feeling. I know my mother only pretends not to be worried about me, and I know I am not there to encourage my younger brothers and sisters in the things that they love. I missed three High School graduations, four birthdays, and America's Independence Day to take this trip. I quit my job, sold everything I had of any value, put school on hold, and hit the road. I didn't know what would come my way. I was just physically tracing out a path of inquisition, of testing myself, removing the familiarity and context of every day life to see what parts of me would stick, and what parts would burn away.

I was becoming more simple, less worrisome, more aware of the magic of life, and no less restless. Many travellers stay gone for so long that they never go home. Their place back home has slowly been filled in by their loved ones with other activities, and other people. The enthusiastic letters of encouragement, the 'I miss you's, all begin to wane, and the telephone conversations decay from excited, connected exchanges between two people that know each other so well, to updates on what is new, each searching for things to say to someone slowly becoming a stranger. I know that this is happening to me, and am determined to have a meaningful journey to bring home to my family and friends, for they are the only thing I love more than the road.

The night train is an environment completely its own, moving forward. While everything else sleeps, our world is still lit up and alive. It's closer to the truth, devoid of boundaries, politics, everyone with no choice but to sit, face to face, simple and pure, really with everything in common. For now, our paths are the same, completely contained in the flourescent light, yellow velour seats, and silver steel trim. Ashtrays are well used, the floors stained and marked, and the soot and residue and energy of the thousands of souls before us gathered in the tiny cracks along the trim. And always that rhythm pulsing up from the tracks, from the center of the earth.

Some immediately try to sleep. Others are reading or talking, and a few get up to wander. One big woman, with a restless face and wild hair, emerges from a cabin for a smoke. She takes a long drag and slowly exhales, and that smell of a lit match fills the hall as she waves it back and forth and flicks it out the window. She never acknowledges me, just stares into the darkness, looks weary. Then for no reason, she puts her head out the window completely, returns with a giant mess of hair, and goes back into her cabin.

I am on the Budapest Special, the overnight from Belgrade, in a cabin with three other travellers: Marko, a young, successful Austrian who is riding the train home because his motorcycle was stolen, Marie, a woman of about 50, and Stela, a girl from Moldova with the most honest blue eyes and delicate smile. She's wearing a pastel pink sweater, with sandy-colored pants and honest shoes and radiates a quiet optimism and a genuine infatuation with all of life's possibilities. She has the posture of a child, folding her legs under her body in her seat next to a window, and smiles with her eyes, looking back and forth at us as we talk. As the train moves through the night, our little cabin is lit and filled with our life stories and struggles. I tell them where I've been, and where I'm going, rattling off names of countries like candy, not realizing that most of these places are out of the question for them. Stela's face lights up.

"I wish I could see all of those places! Someday Moldovans won't need visas to enter and I might be able to take a trip like that!"

I would have given her every experience and journey I ever had.

Marie, a doctor on her way home from a short trip to Italy, has four suitcases full of books to carry home from the station. Her kind, round face, and sweet voice are even more so, framed by a short halo of dishwater-gold curls, and clothed in modest flowered blouse and neutral trousers, with hands clasped in her lap. Her wise, blue eyes, sparkling, with laugh lines radiating around them, and her head thoughtfully tilted, she tells us of the fragmentation of Yugoslavia, and the conflicts immediately after.

"It was almost like Heaven back then. We all had plenty of money and everything we needed. Then it all vanished."

Her expression changes to sadness for a moment, then regains its intensity and hope.

"We have been through a lot, and all this fighting for no reason, but things are getting better, slowly".

Marie, wrestling around those heavy bags, having to be ready for a full day's work in only a few hours, tough as anyone who has experienced war, has a content soul that comes from knowing, really knowing that life hangs by a thread, always. Marko and I help Marie off the train, and watch her wise and gentle figure disappear through the window of our cabin. Marko has long since stopped talking about his motorcycle.

Stela has a similar story of growing up in Moldova, a child watching the Soviet Union crumble around her. She's going to school in Serbia for European studies.

"Moldova wants to joint the EU, and I want to be a part of it. There is a lot to do before they will consider us".

Moldovans have taken quite a ride in the past years. After the fall of the Soviet Union, they watched as their economy fell to be the weakest in Europe. Those in power couldn't agree on a Western view or continued alignment with Russia, and to this day, Russia continues to influence Moldovan elections by illegally distributing literature and broadcasting propaganda. Many are striving to meet standards for joining the EU, but in demonstrations, some EU flag wavers have been arrested for "anti-nationalism". I secretly marvelled at their pure dedication and work ethic amid such a massive situation. There is nothing I wrestle with more than how small I am in the universe.

The train pulls forward, with an engineer we never see, out of our control, forging ahead, with or without us. It is up to the passenger to get on or off and choose opportunities, make contact. Not without its share of thieves and liars, but overflowing with the good travellers of life, ready to share a story, a piece of bread, and maybe even some good wine, as a picture book of our times rolls by the windows, the night train is a rare invitation to peak into lives, and souls, and dark corners of the world, and ourselves.

If only our leaders could speak so candidly with one another. We all want the same things: To live and let live, to go wherever on this planet we feel compelled, to interact with others and learn from them, their histories. Humanity continues to fragment into different nations, with our leaders and ambassadors to speak for us, but I wonder if in those meetings the same level of head nodding, empathetic looks, elbows on knees, and expressions of wonder and realization take place. Why can we, the vast majority of average somebodies in the world get along just fine, but become hostile and paranoid once a few lines are drawn across a map and a label affixed?

Tens of millions of us have slaughtered one another over the squabbles and hunger of a very small few, all of us just wanting to live, eat, sleep, have a laugh every now and then, continually dragged into the middle of all the things we are trying to forget, and maybe that's the real problem. We're looking away, heads in the sand, hearts unable to absorb all the hurt and absurdity in the world. War makes about as much sense as two fleas fighting over a football field.

The train is pulling into the station now, our journey together over, and new ones just beginning. The dawn has broken and is glowing gold, lighting up the tracks like strips of neon, and streaming in from the windows high above in the arched ceiling of the Budapest station. Everyone is scattering in a frenzy of luggage, kisses hello, hugs goodbye, the commotion echoing throughout the entire building, with the rattle of the cars, and the ticking of the signs changing destinations: Beograd, L'Viv, Vienna, Warszawa, Bucharesti, Praha.

Our common line is now splitting a thousand directions, like a dandelion blown with a child's breath. We are all brothers and sisters, each of us with a burning inside us, making our way in this crazy old world, businessmen, old ladies, children, in a Heaven of mistakes, broken hearts, new beginnings, spilled wine, in a whirlpool of all of it, each bruise an invitation, every failure an open door, each new person a teacher, with our mountains to climb and tumble down the other side. I am stumbling through the station with my pack over a shoulder, and out into the beauty of day, with more questions than answers, but knowing that this journey is a just one, wishing more could take it.

Neruda Visits Idaho

Ron McFarland

Cindy from the state humanities council
tells us she thinks Pablo Neruda
visited Idaho once, probably Boise,
maybe back in the Sixties,
but I see him elsewhere in the state
potato famous on its license plates,
and great for sugar beets, trout streams,
ski runs, and the River of No Return.

I see Neruda in Nampa at Wal-Mart
buying a pair of cut-rate Wranglers
and sunglasses he'll lose in Buhl
at the Dairy Queen, where he writes
post cards back to Santiago, Chile,
and an elemental ode to napkins.
Offered the opportunity to read at
Sun Valley, Pablo passes, in his
proletarian way, and hurries off
east to Twin Falls in search
of figureheads clipped from the tall ships.

Of course Neruda must be disappointed
not to find so much as a bare-chested
mermaid there, or in Chubbock,
or even in the greater Pocatello
metropolitan area. In Rexburg Pablo
soon learns that Chilean red does not

suggest good wine, but bad politics.
Looking back on it in Isla Negra,
Neruda writes one love poem,
twenty songs of despair.

As of Yet
James Grinwis

He didn't know what made him leap in front of the oncoming car. It was swerving around the bend near the fitness club. Shiny, black, luminescent as if streaked with rain though it was ninety degrees and sunny out, the car came, globe-shaped headlights like two porcupine fishes. Strange, the people inside, a man and a woman, looked exactly alike. They were small and elderly. The man's hand clutched the steering wheel in perfect ten and two o'clock positioning. His hands resembled his headlights, shriveled yet glowing with an ancient, embedded warmth.

He jumped because it felt at the time that it was what he wanted to do. He'd gone drinking the other night and felt tired. Life was going pretty well for him actually. Promotion. Vacation coming up. Relationship solidly in place, except for minor details that if not considered objectively, with intelligence, could shake the foundation out of it. But he was generally an objective and intelligent man. So it wasn't because of anything that he jumped in front of the oncoming car which had, to be quite fair, absolutely no time to react.

He hit the left side of the hood and his limbs crumpled over it briefly before being flung into the gravel of the road. His clothing, including both shoes, was torn off of him. The whole right side of his skin was stripped onto the road, making it seem like a section of one of those smelly Moroccan tanneries. Some minutes flew by, everything was still. Sirens began to light up the distance. Some people, he perceived, were approaching, pushing wheelbarrows, shovels, big elastic garbage bags, and metal buckets of soapy water. It didn't look like they came from the mouth of an ambulance, but from somewhere else, somewhere farther down the road.

A Jesus Shirt
James Grinwis

My brother comes home from the job he is about to lose, ladles the first of his evening beers from the brew pot, takes a shower out back, and puts on his Jesus shirt.

The Jesus shirt is blue with white letters stretched across its front, something about a Cross Country championship from 1978. It has been around for thirty years.

According to him, there is no longer any championship in my brother, and I watch him as I sip from the cup of broth our mother has made for me. He is lean, like a tonsil, and a scowl is always plastered to his face.

My brother has escorted, for years, the muse of crumbling. Her name is Cissy, and he has bedded her, in fact. The Jesus shirt is ripped in places, and has many holes, some ferocious looking, as if a wild animal had stuck itself to it. Thus is their love-making. Its noise is the sound of a squeaky violin.

It throws forth a huge, ancient light that cascades over everything and fills us with weird warmth.

"You will soar again soon," I say to him, "and I will find the right light to pluck for you." In the bulb of his head I hear snow falling.

The Ferry Business
James Grinwis

Life these days wasn't that great for Charon and his team. Little warriors and minstrels wanting a ride all the time. Business was never meant to be this good.

When the clown came to fill out an application, ferryman 4 looked him over with a dubiousness bordering on rage. "I just don't like that stupid grin," mumbled 4, "plus, in uniform, he'll look like a fool." Still, Charon accepted the application with his brittle hand, folded it in his breast pocket, and creaked over to Personnel, a warm glow emanating from his gnarly balloon of a head.

Times were changing. Wanda, of professional services, hissed with looser amounts of static. The master didn't seem to be as ominous as before, he just sort of limped around. It was time for a new boss, someone thought a moment, before squelching.

The clown donned his new musk ox cloak, and got into a spare boat. He began to carve smiley faces into the planks.

Seven Lost Thoughts of Highly Effective People
James Grinwis

1)
"I have my poems to keep me warm," the executive remembered, putting the last of his personal effects in the last of his retirement boxes, hearing the wind-chill splinter against his ears.

2)
The call was cold. She did not move against the chairs. "The flower arrangements back in Avignon..."

3)
The salad greens were yellow. The air smelled of oxtail soup. The space between losing and winning. "Where I live," the politician mumbled.

4)
She made so many mental notes, her eyes were razors made of blueberries. She was her own mechanical universe, her own orrery. "Wish someone would spin me..."

5)
Sakuteiki: the oldest treatise on landscape gardening. Islands in a pond should resemble strands of mist. Like a star system. "I read massive amounts of works and don't know what to do about it."

6)
With the impudence of the young juggernaut, the technician fixed his attention elsewhere. "The greenish foam of March. Up or down is everything."

7)
"There are no strange invaders in the shed. It is something I strive for, this sterile pasture." The medicine man mused on a revolving door in the place of stone tablets.

A Blue Circus
James Grinwis

The buffoonery clicks. The absurdists are all in sync together. It is January, when the gold light of dusty paintings rubs itself onto surfboards.

The circus arrives at the town of Sprout's Lick. Fimby, the manager, looks out at the desolate crowd. He had yet to bring his troupe to as somber a place as this, a place where humor had been sucked dry, it seems.

The sun, like a giant mouth, chews apart the earth. Mud snow spurts out of it and dusts the frozen cabbages.

The bard churns out three new seductions to meet the challenge, and the dancers weave new corsets and hair ribbons, though there is a suspicious feeling permeating the tent that the audience would be happier watching a starving bobcat set loose in the house of reptiles, small children and ferns.

The Spell of Love

Michael Maschio

Karem found his mother in the kitchen. She was smiling the crying smile of the dead-wishing-not-to-be-dead, with bubbles of spit occupying a lost tooth's pink gap and gray dust drying her eyes.

Where were the men who had murdered her?

"In Najaf," guessed Karem.

They had waited for his older brothers, Sayed and Hassan, to leave for work; then had entered his home and slapped his mother and beaten his father clumsily with a fallen pot (his father, Abbas, lay unconscious now with his bare legs sticking out of the bedroom); then they had beaten Karem's chest and shoulder with a rifle butt.

How many men had there been?

"Five. More. I couldn't see."

Masked, they had exposed their chins and mouths to spit on him (for having tried to stand); then they had retracted and spread his legs and raped him, punching him about his head and stomach, such that now, without pants, wearing a dust-streaked shirt, he knelt beside his mother with his bruised ribcage tenderized by gasp and shudder. Mariam was thirty-two: her chin as pointy as her pinpoint nose and her blackened third tooth matching her mole. Her hair, having come undone, resembled a grasping hand.

Where were the five hundred Japanese soldiers charged with protecting Samawa?

"At . . . their base," cried Karem.

The Japanese soldiers were renovating the hospital (as well as working on water purification), whereas Karem's brothers were painting the hospital, beautifying baked concrete walls with scenes of life and liberation. The murderers, meanwhile, were members of either the Mahdi Army or the Badr Organization, rival Shiite militias.

Which?

"I don't know."

His mother's gray nose matched her gray cheeks and palms (she had shielded her face when they had kicked dust on her) and her blood was black and waxy. Karem, re-hearing her prayers (uttered at her last moment), rejoined them now despairingly with a tottering head and cracking voice.

Since 2003, British, Dutch and Australian soldiers had been protecting Samawa. In 2004, Japanese soldiers had arrived to reconstruct existing buildings and build a sewer system; but in December, Koichi Kato, a Japanese politician, had told the *New York Times*, "They went there claiming that they will contribute to reconstruction, but they have hardly been able to get the work done . . . There is no reason for them to be there. The place is not safe, and it is impossible to do reconstruction."

Tasting his own blood, Karem could not swallow. Neither could he survey the property damage, let alone gauge his father's health.

Why had he not revived his father?

"He can't see me like this."

His father would be transfixed by his mother's disemboweled body, overwrought by misery and silenced by enmity, and only secondarily concerned about Karem.

"He can't know."

Karem meant his father could not know he had been raped. With pulsing eyes, he returned to his bedroom and stepped into pants, hopping choppily, battering the doorframe.

Had he glanced at his father?

"No."

Standing with his head tipped toward his mother's gruesome wound, he asked for Allah's help in whispered mantra, and futilely queried, "Oh, God, why?" before collapsing against the wall, hiding his face in his hand, favoring his left side. Martyrs were free when they died for Islam, when they died for eternal life, when their blood was immaculate (meaning innocent), and when they were free of this sad world, but his mother was not a martyr. She was a victim.

Was she free?

"I . . . I don't want to say goodbye."

He had repeated "Why?" not "Goodbye" through tears and moans.

"I won't say it."

Yet he would curse the murderers and avenge her murder, be unwise and remain in Samawa, kill insurgents and die, never marry and have children, but die along with his father and brothers, rudely and very soon.

"We'll kill them."

Lying three feet from a pillow, stiff, concussed and beckoning death, his father was too weak to kill anyone, whereas Karem, shaking his head no, no and cupping his chin, palmed a slimy layer of mucous and tears.

His enemies had defeated him.

Was he ashamed?

"Yes."

His enemies were hypocrites and worldly oppressors.

Which set had done this to his family?

"They both did it."

The leader of the Mahdi Army was Moktada al-Sadr; the leader of the Bahr Organization was Hadi Al-Amiri. Each militia was working with criminals as well as the Coalition and Iran. Had the Coalition targeted his family? Had criminals? Had Iran? Which Shiite militia had done this?

"All of them."

No one had done this – no one he knew or would ever find.

"I swear by Allah . . ."

Allah had done this – or had let it happen, and Karem's swearing was meaningless. Beside his parents' bedroom door was a stove with a rounded white border beneath wooden shelves supporting a basin, pots, cups and additional cooking paraphernalia. The kitchen's highest shelf, also its smallest, balanced a decoratively upended basket displaying a woven green starburst. A narrow white shelf, also undisturbed, displayed postcard-sized photographs of his bearded father and brothers. Surveying these, then closing his eyes, he tried to determine who had come to their home, literally the very men whose punitive, desirous sounds still burned his nostrils, ears, fingertips, anus and eyes.

He wanted to stay here and he wanted what had happened not to have happened, but could he stay here – could his family – even with Allah's protection?

"Yes . . . Yes!"

He shook his head no, no, dropping his hands and leaning forward, exchanging his chin for his mother's: cupping it caringly while avoiding her bloody abaya; then, starkly, he found his father's youthful face amid her smile lines – her sole wrinkles – the jovial face his father would routinely summon upon seeing her. In actuality, his father's face was acutely weak, gaunt and non-authoritative. Had Karem assessed it, he would have concluded nothing could be done.

"My father will help."

When his mother had been a girl, his father had taken her in. Sayed and Hassan were brothers by another wife who had been murdered in 1991. Sayed and Hassan had not avenged their mother and would not avenge Karem's mother.

"They will."

They would console Karem, but not risk their lives for a woman their junior. Indeed, their limited love for her was as functional as the tiny table opposite her and Karem, with its dusty tablecloth and bucket for washing vegetables. The Japanese would not help. The British, Dutch and Australians would not help. The U.S. would not help. The Coalition believed Iraq had nothing to offer but oil and military bases. Islam was a religion of a defeated people. Golden Age achievements had been trumped by modernism and contemporary science and Iraqi Muslims now were worth no more than the dusty land they occupied.

Karem uttered, "There is no God but Allah. There is no..."

An hour later, Capt. Nayef Jasem uttered the same conviction, albeit sympathetically. Capt. Jasem was a family friend and former Revolutionary Guard, now a policeman. He questioned Karem while three officers shrouded Karem's mother's body; then the officers carried Karem's father to an ambulance. His father would be admitted to the hospital and his brothers located and informed, whereas his mother's body would be taken to the morgue.

Karem, disclaiming tears, detailed the crime and omitted the rape. He affirmed Capt. Jasem's promise of justice. Capt. Jasem planned to search for witnesses and detain suspects.

"Someone will know," he assured Karem.

Capt. Jasem was sharp-nosed and round-faced, making him astutely handsome, with a close beard and even teeth, in contrast to Karem, whose large black eyes and oversized head of loopy hair, and general slightness, made him topsy and frail. During boyhood, Capt. Jasem had played with Karem's brothers, and Capt. Jasem's family had known Karem's mother long before she had married Karem's father. Wearing dark blue pants and a light blue shirt, Capt. Jasem put on his beret and said he would notify her family. He took Karem along.

Traversing Samawa, Karem sensed the understanding of onlookers despite their ignorance of what had happened. The street was elderly blue, the palm trees and other trees fervently grouped or decoratively aligned and the slopes and breaks throughout the perimeter sidewalks dust-swept or dust-filled. The hospital resembled a baked sandcastle set against the bluest of skies with narrative wall paintings both colorful and positive, albeit an unfinished Japanese matron offering sustenance to a juvenile Iraqi mother conveyed the unfortunate stop-and-start pattern of the beautification project.

Sayed and Hassan had not shown up for work. Capt. Jasem, suspecting the worst, questioned their fellow painters vigorously, while Karem, off to the side, suffered what little hope he had to repeat on him like a vomit reflex. His brothers were dead, or so he determined.

Why was this happening?

"We're being punished."

They were not being punished; they were being victimized.

"No. No!"

He wanted to avenge the crimes he had witnessed, the crime he had experienced and the crime he was now dreading. The hospital's unpainted walls replicated his vitality: facing them flattened him, such that he was ready to act, yet no one cared what he would do. Even he did not care.

"I do. I do!"

Yet he did not know what to do.

"My father will help."

His unconscious father, bedridden and ebbing, was too old to help – and he might not survive.

Where were the murderers?

"I don't know. I don't know!"

Karem would never find them.

"I will kill them!"

His mother was dead, his brothers probably dead and his father nearly dead. Even Karem's dreary life had been viciously degraded.

Capt. Jasem told him, "Stay with my family until I find the ones that did this. My family will be your family. I swear to Allah. I will take your brothers' place. I will be a good son to your father and you will be a good brother to me."

"I want to find them."

"No, Karem, I'll find them."

"I want to come with you."

"No. My family will take care of you. You're part of my family now."

Karem would not say yes.

Capt. Jasem said, "Go to my home. Go."

Karem would not go.

On the way to the police station, Capt. Jasem halted beside a tuft of grass flared toward the Euphrates River. He tasseled Karem's head of loops with an embrace resembling a headlock and whispered endearments and pledges, begging him home, where Capt. Jasem's wife, Fatima, would feed him, but Karem would not leave.

Australian and Iraqi soldiers guarded the police station. Inside, officers in blue shirts and soldiers in fatigues jointly executed Iraq's version of community policing: i.e. routing insurgents and protecting humanitarian projects. Many officers here had trained in Jordan in heavy arms and human rights, albeit vigilante justice, severely punishable, persisted due to the frequent release of guilty prisoners (by the Coalition). For instance, photographs of police officers on cell phones recently sufficed as evidence of terrorism, such that police officers beat to death with donkey sticks three men and critically injured two more. Even Capt. Jasem had killed insurgents and suspected insurgents. Generally, Iraqis in Samawa trusted the police, but infiltration by Iranian intelligence (cash payments to induce Coalition withdrawal and enforce strict Islamic law), and securitization for the upcoming election (for a transitional government tasked with writing a constitution) were increasing altercations among the population, the police and insurgent groups, particularly Sunnis, who were being killed, displaced and oppressed.

Seated in a back room, facing an empty cell amid file cabinets serving Capt. Jasem and other officers, Karem fell asleep. His dream of relief and denial domed his brain like a solstice, but soon voices tightened his breathing and awoke him. The voices belonged to the murderers.

Had they returned?

"No. Please, no."

Or had he come to them?

"What?"

The murderers were in the front room, cavorting, possibly working, not locked in the cell, hopeless and meek, as would befit prisoners.

Karem was shaking. "Is this . . . a dream?"

He was not dreaming. The murderers were police officers. Why had they murdered his mother? Why had they beaten his father? Why had they murdered his brothers, if his brothers had been murdered? Why had they abused him?

"It's not them."

The voices of the murderers matched the voices of the police officers: identical grunts and guffaws, cryptic repartee. Crouched, Karem peered between the door and its frame. The station's activity was ordinary. He recognized only the three officers who had accompanied Capt. Jasem, while his pain, worsening, further tightened his breathing. His next breath was shallow. Soon he would be panting.

Where had the murderers gone?

"It's not them."

Where was Capt. Jasem?

"I don't see him."

Perhaps Capt. Jasem and the murderers were out patrolling, or perhaps Karem was hearing voices that did not exist.

"They're somewhere. They're somewhere and we'll find them."

His brothers had disappeared. Capt. Jasem was busy with other operations. Who was "we"?

"Saafa will help."

Saafa's father would keep Saafa home.

"And Ahmed."

The same went for Ahmed's father.

Karem sat on the floor. An officer entered the back room and filed paperwork before spotting him. The officer was young and stout with two moles on his cheek. He closed a filing cabinet and lowered his arms; his shirt's black buttons remained taut and, between these buttons, his shirt's diamond-gaps revealed his stomach.

Did Karem recognize the moles?

"I couldn't see their faces."

The officer asked Karem if he was all right. Did Karem recognize the officer's voice?

"I'm all right," lied Karem.

The officer, doubtful, paused; then thought better and walked out. Karem followed him and exited the station. He would return to the hospital, see his father and solicit his advice. The street was busy, but crackling gunshots cleared it. Leaving his sandals behind, Karem hid behind a gate. He wanted to return to the station – for the gunshots to be his, directed throughout the station. Pressing his crown against the gate enabled him to focus on the head-sized hexagonal stone directly between his feet: chipped, pale and mud-packed. He wanted to be dead, if being dead meant being with his mother, and he wanted the murderers dead, too, even if such would entail his death – and if the murderers were somehow to live, he did not want to live.

Why, then, had he left the station?

"Because they . . . they won't ever . . ."

He meant they would never rape him again.

Pressing his crown and closing his eyes, he considered the hollow clang the gate would emit were he to butt it or fall back and kick it and kick it, and even absent such actions, the hollow clang reverberated beneath his neck, such that he realized, finally, not the gate, but his heart was clanging. He held his breath, muting his heartbeat, and believed he could die. Hatred, indignity and absence should have broken the spell of love, but love was the sole ordinate withstanding his confusion, yet he did not know what to do.

"I know what to do."

He was doing nothing, yet felt love. Did he want to stop feeling love?

"No . . . no!"

He rubbed his head yes, yes, against the gate. His mother, only yesterday afternoon, had checked a water bucket's level.

The bucket, in the bathtub, had contained seventeen minutes of trickle, requiring boiling, but now she was dead. She had lit a candle last night (they had only had two hours of electricity), pursing her lips due to the match's heat, but now she was dead. He heard his father compiling complaints just as he had done last night, but his father was dying and soon would be dead. He felt his brothers lift him by his arms, just as jocularly as they always would, but his brothers . . . and his home: it was no longer a home.

What was his love worth now?

"I don't know, but . . . it won't stop . . ."

Love exceeded his hunger and shame, betrayal, bereavement and hatred. He wanted too much to happen, right now, yet was aimless.

To whom could he turn for help?

"I . . . I have no one."

He had been attending school and working part-time at the cement factory. Now he would neither work nor return to school. His family barely existed. The hexagonal stone between his feet buttressed an identical stone. Were he to follow the stones back toward the house, he would note their dip and disappearance in dark mud.

Was this path his past or future?

"I know what I'm going to do."

He did not know. The Bahr Organization, in the guise of the police, had killed his mother for adultery: she had maintained a long relationship with another man, perhaps Capt. Jasem. Karem knew she loved another man. He did not want to know more. In lieu of the hospital, he returned to his house, where he slept in his parents' bed. The murder of his brothers – his sole dream – replayed with each brother dying in the other's arms. Soon, Iraqis would celebrate Eid al-Adha, when submission to Allah is affirmed and an animal sacrificed. When Karem awoke, he cleaned up what the police had left untouched; then stood in the doorway of his house, where he was invaded by shame. By now, everyone knew what had been done to his family, and the rape – the rape had escalated into a murder, in that rape is the murder of someone that lives with a diminished desire to participate in life, someone who will be shunned and ultimately have to accept communal inconsequence.

The succeeding days were merely days, but the nights – the nights were fearsome, for their insomnia, tears, isolation and hopelessness – for their torture.

95

Nothing to Declare
Rachel Newcomb

Red dragon kites splash across a sooty sky, soaring over the heads of children who chase after the pigeons closer to earth. The moment I step off the bus, vendors swarm, thrusting postcards and cheap Mao watches in my face. From his portrait looking out over Tiananmen Square, Mao presides over the commerce, wearing the half-smile of someone who's just discovered a surprise party in his honor but is none too happy about it.

Today I'm on a pilgrimage. I've seen the tombs of Lenin and Ho Chi Minh, so after this I'll have the complete set. So far my greater ambitions for China lie unfulfilled. I was hoping for a religious experience, but I know not to look in the likely places. Let others fall into peyote trances with shamans in Brazil or squat with African *imams* inside mud-brick mosques in Mali. I bypassed the Buddhist temple yesterday, resisting the smoke curling up from burning bundles of incense.

Outside Mao's tomb an efficient line snakes around the building. Police bark commands through a megaphone. The tomb is laid out on a north-south axis, like all the great buildings in China. Even communists believe in *feng shui*.

There is nothing auspicious about being dead, someone behind me is saying. I face forward, avoiding English. I didn't come here to listen to my own kind.

In front of me, a family of peasants, hands gnarled with the evidence of real work. The husband clutches a yellow flower bought from one of the vendors outside. His wife holds an unsmiling, dumpling-faced baby over her shoulder. We enter the mausoleum, a red carpet ending at the foot of a giant marble statue of Mao. Running to the foot of the statue, the father drops his plastic-wrapped flower onto a pile with thousands of identical flowers. He bows three times, merging back with the moving crowd.

They say that Mao was seventy percent right, thirty percent wrong. English again, a male voice answering my thoughts. I turn around and see a respectable looking character, about my age, not bad looking. White *guayabera* straight out of a Cuban fashion show, shaggy brown hair, a beard. Just the type my parents would have chosen for me. He doesn't meet my eyes.

In addition to seeking nirvana, on this trip I'm revisiting some of my earlier career plans. Baton twirler. *Solid Gold* dancer. Astronaut. The future soaring above me in kites that are not yet in my hands.

I'm afraid to disappoint you that Solid Gold's not on anymore.

I wasn't speaking, but somehow the man has found a way to respond. I chalk it up to the Magic of Mao.

What is it about growing up that sucks away desire like a vacuum, leaving life airless, sterile? On birthdays I used to wish for Barbies with hard plastic torpedoes for breasts. Instead I got gender-neutral dolls, macrobiotic gardening kits for children. I wanted strict bed times, not activist friends who came over on school nights and stayed up late drinking and ranting about the Sandinistas, leaving wine stains on the battered Danish coffee table. All this makes it hard to be satisfied with convention.

Suddenly Mao is beside us. He's lying on my right, higher than the crowd filing by, encased in glass. His face glows unnaturally beneath the lights, although what's natural about being dead and on display for thirty years? I try not to think of my father. He wanted open-casket, wanted people to see him as a poster child for his causes, his face sunken in from cancer that mushroomed out of twenty years of living near a nuclear plant. He hoped his funeral would inspire people to revolt against the things that hurt him. The military-industrial complex, big dams, pesticides, carbon emissions, wars for oil, cold wars, the OJ Simpson trial, child labor, Rwandan genocide, thexploitationofthethirdworldforitsresources, the murder of Patrice Lumumba, colonialism, the fall of the Berlin Wall and what he feared would come after. What he missed: global warming, hydrogenated oils, sexed-up baby dolls in pageants, outsourcing, the death of Princess Di, theexploitationofhthethirdworldforitslabor, even China opening itself up to unfettered capitalism.

I read in a biography that Mao wasn't fond of baths. He just liked to be sponged down with a wet towel. His personal physician claimed that this led many of his mistresses to catch VD.

The hotel bathroom offers sanitized cloths wrapped in plastic. On the package it says, "Use after sex. Prevents spread of disease."

I'm thinking about how these guys messed it up for the rest of us. Mao, Nasser, Castro. There must have been a time when it was possible not to live with this consciousness of how the great dreams were all going to lead to suffering.

The crowd nearly stops, and the guards are shouting for us to move along. In front of me the baby wails, longing for milk. The father wipes his eyes; is he crying too? The swaying crowd shoves me against the family, and I become intimately acquainted with the scratchy warp of man's polyester coat, made to look like wool. Up close he smells of tobacco. I can feel myself panicking. Wish I'd taken the Xanax today. It calms me in small spaces. But then there's a protective American arm around my body, a hand pulling me away from the family. I don't turn around, but I can hear his thoughts. Mao fills him with wonder, with big, answerless questions.

Are good intentions good enough? All my suffering is self-inflicted. Poems and sympathy and the dollar a day we throw at the television for starving kids with toothpicks for legs and empty gourds for bellies is far from enough. I'm calling for a radical redistribution of the wealth. Sure, I wouldn't benefit. They'd take it all away from me—my restored Karmann Ghia, my father's Elgin pocket watch. Nights at the multiplex drooling over a Bond movie and a ten dollar box of nachos. A million books at my fingertips on the Internet, and nobody forbidding me to read Chomsky. I need to be happy with less. I think I could live with nothing except my memories. Those I would hoard, to pull out secretly at night, under the covers, when I reflected on the sweetness of all the things I'd lost.

The crowd heaves forward, the arm slips away, and I'm breathing the smell of strangers again.

Chalk off Dictator Corpse #3. In the gift shop there are coins, compasses and fans, Mao magnets and stamps, in case I want to commemorate it. Later, for dinner I go for the Beijing duck, slabs of greasy meat wrapped in pancakes with scallions and a sweet sauce. Tomorrow I fly away from all this. On the plane ride back I hear him again, a few seats away from me, the constant hum of thoughts disquieted by China.

We'll always have Mao. He wills me to turn around. His irony has a subtext; I can imagine what he really wants: himself behind me again, a disembodied voice pressed up against mine. What would I find if I turned around? Shared pilgrimages to the places that mark what's left of other people's big dreams. Someone to hear my thoughts. Someone I can be with, and still be absolutely alone. *We have so much in common.* We should be together. I smile inwardly, hoping my smile mirrors everything that is possible.

Mexico, Midsummer
Sandra M. Castillo

I bounce off the surface of this blue stretch, another life splashing saltwater kisses on my face, searching for something in your voice, but you are at Daddy O's, pulsing, sweating to sporadic lights, blasts of ice falling down your body as you twirl to the alcohol inside you, laughing to the impulsive rhythms of anonymous bodies, dancing in a blood-warm room, touching strangers in a familiar darkness connecting us all, your body wet with sweat pouring into the Mexican dawn like a blood sacrifice.

Amor loco. Amor brujo

The blistering touch of summer skin, I turn into myself, knowing that across the street of coincidence, you are closing your eyes to this tiny island, to the blue that has always surrounded us, to my mouth and my eyes, the fear of recognition beating against your chest, your memory.

Otras vidas. Otros tiempos.

The Chosen Ones
Gary Glauber

Through small acts of defiance, we subversives aim to awaken the slumbering masses to the insidious reality of this government's fascist machine. Our current plan would do just that. It's a sound plan and one that needs doing. I have no issue with that. My problem is with Nate Chamberlain.

Back in Schwarzenegger High, Chamberlain was my nemesis. I remember one day he approached with his usual smirk and swagger.

"Yo Pengar," he said. "I challenge you to a contest. Let's see who can punch the softest...you go first."

I fell for the bait, delivering a mere whisper of a glance. I barely touched his arm.

Then Chamberlain said, "My turn."

Before I had time to react, he wound up and delivered the most powerful, hardest punch I'd ever taken. My arm was throbbing for hours after.

"I lose," he said, skipping down the hall toward his next victim as I fought back tears.

Another time Chamberlain wrested what had been a corner of a red flannel shirt sticking out of a gym locker until the whole article was unloosed and in his possession. He then invited onlookers to join him in defacing the shirt. He ripped off buttons, mangled a sleeve, then watched as some boys tossed it into the running shower. To Chamberlain, this wasn't enough.

He fetched the soaked shirt's remains and threw it in one of the urinals. He then challenged everyone in the gym class to pee on it. It became a matter of some urgency for each boy to do so, rather than be called "a gutless wimp of a pussy" by Chamberlain. In turn, each of us had to shake one off on the drenched red flannel. I took my spot and delivered a solid yellow stream of teenage acceptance.

What I didn't acknowledge was that it was my shirt. Yet it was fairly obvious when I spent the rest of the day wearing nothing but my white cotton undershirt. I bet Chamberlain knew it was mine. To this day, his nettlesome snicker still echoes in some dark recess of my brain.

That was ages ago. I went on to college and grad school, became Daniel Pengar, a fairly successful programmer, inventor and civil engineer. Nathan Chamberlain joined the armed forces, leaving behind the thrill of the thrown brick, the glow of the successful shoplift. After a few tours of duty, he returned to the old neighborhood, finally garnering the respect that had eluded his delinquent youth.

But my background dossier says respect didn't translate into employment or happiness. Chamberlain was down on his luck – going from bad to worse in a swift succession of petty failures, fired from bad jobs, dismissed from even worse relationships. He grew depressed, became overweight, desperate and pathetic, living at rock bottom.

Then (according to a recent magazine interview) Chamberlain had some sort of an epiphany. "While scavenging dumpsters in search of edible food," he said, "I came across a book that changed my life." It was some archaic self-help treatise by an obscure author long before Chamberlain's time. "Those words nourished my troubled soul more than any five-course meal," he said. "It showed me I had been happiest when in service to others." He then recounted his military experience, and how glad he was to represent our nation overseas.

Chamberlain swears the book changed his attitude. It sparked the necessary discipline for change. By all accounts, that metamorphosis has been nothing short of miraculous. Chamberlain's now the poster boy for clean, healthy living. A strict regimen of weightlifting, cardio-exercise and reasonable diet improved his appearance. In storybook fashion, Chamberlain lucked into a lucrative modeling career. His body and face now are familiar to many through high-profile work in fashion underwear and toiletry ads. He even gets magazine interviews.

The government (more specifically, the ministry of communication and entertainment) also recognizes his potential. They've selected Chamberlain as the male component on the upcoming season of their very popular television reality show "The Chosen Ones." His chosen companion will be a very lovely specimen as well, one Alyssa Manitoba. However, it'll be another sub's job to handle her; I'm the lucky guy assigned Chamberlain.

*   *   *   *   *

In its first two seasons "The Chosen Ones" set records, both for viewership and overall audience approval. The ratings went through the roof, particularly the separate pay-per-view "adults-only" segments. The premise of the show is simple enough – two ideal specimens are chosen from the population at large, one male, one female. Allegedly, there is science behind the selection, their likely chemistry calculated beforehand. What's most obvious is their attractive appearance – there's no mistaking the vanity aspect. These are living dolls – Barbie meets G.I. Joe – and they voluntarily pair up as a couple under the 'round-the-clock scrutiny of field cameras. They are given the equivalent of a royal life for the extent of a television season (13 weeks). Then, in a somewhat bizarre voyeuristic twist, the season closes with the couple being offered as human sacrifice. According to the show's producers, this "gift to God" is what our great nation is all about, an ultimate act of selfless love and sacrifice.

103

We humble subversives view this as senseless murder dressed in fancy clothing, the same type of reckless killing our government enacts the world over. Of course, speculation in the media debates whether or not these sacrifices are real. We subs have conducted our own research – and it's the genuine deal. The four predecessors from seasons one and two are no longer, except in reruns and eventual syndication. Captured for eternity in digital images, they had their fifteen minutes of virtual fame and then were literally served up like veal calves to slaughter.

Each season starts with an episode introducing the two principals. These two are put up (by government funding) in some luxury accommodation, usually a fancy beach house whose massive well-decorated interiors resemble those found in spacious European manors, except each room seems to have a hot tub.

Usually, there's a hastened period of adjustment wherein the principals get to know one another. Once that's accomplished, the show truly begins. Everyone loves a love story and that's where "The Chosen Ones" thrives. Ordinary men and women live vicariously through watching these two paradigms of pulchritude get it on.

At first, there's flirting. Eventually, there's passion. And, for an extra $39.95, people can order a special "adults only" segment broadcast over pay-per-view cable. This alone generates record revenues for the government's ministry of communication and entertainment.

The show's participants are asked to do little more than enjoy this cushy life that's been thrust upon them. They're waited on hand and foot, given personal trainers and private chefs, allowed any type of luxury or activity desired.

Those chosen are naturally dynamic folks, athletic, enthusiastic and brimming with a visual charisma that commands one's attention. These are the men and women we wish we'd become, thrown together for an opulent, decadent fling with the public as witness. It sates our innate proclivities toward natural beauty, romance, prurient interest and gossip.

As an adoring public looks on, this couple lives life to the fullest en route to the startling conclusion of death via sacrifice. No matter how repulsive and/or unethical this idea might seem, there's no denying it's good television!

*   *   *   *   *

There is no answer to this apprehension that assaults me. I must confront the bully. Stare my past intimidator in the face and try to rescue him.

I try visualizing exercises, turning the other proverbial cheek over and over in my mind, talking it through against my very uncivil inclinations.

I wrestle with myself, my too silent savior, and the memories of past humiliations borne uneasily. Was it just hatred – or was there a part of me that marveled at his raw power and lack of remorse? Did I ever wish that was me for an instant, the rogue force, reveling in the pile of shame delivered relentlessly in deserted school corridors, quiet alleyways, and in the fearful ears of peers? The boy could, by his very presence, turn a peaceful park's bucolic arbor into an open air torture chamber. Ah, to wield such terror, to elicit enough timorous tears to fill a proud basin as if this was a great and worthy accomplishment: I have a neighborhood swimming with fear.

We quaked in our boots then, hearts racing, caught up in little dramas of debasement. A young population reduced to cowering and kowtowing to this false idol of belligerence. Nate was our catalyst, he who set the nightmares to racing across waking days. I despised him and yet, admired the purity of evil in his delinquent acts, a universe apart from my plain life of small academic achievements and relative obedience.

He had given me and a legion of others the gift of true fear. Yet from this sprang the inner bile that churned and did not settle. Rather, it has goaded me on to a lifetime of tenacious rebellion for the common good, a noble quest against bullies everywhere.

Soon I must step forth to face this devil, extend a willing hand to pull him from the government's even greater, more forceful hell. Past enemy, befriend me. He who has taunted and haunted me, let me save you now.

I take ten deep breaths and start again. Nate, forgive my personal enmity. I release our past for the sake of the future. Let us join forces and be victorious. Please.

*　　*　　*　　*　　*

A few subs have arranged for this "casual" meeting with Chamberlain. He hasn't yet been publicly announced as next season's contestant (but we're acting on reliable inside information). He's sunbathing in a chaise lounge at poolside, a sculpted bronze Adonis comfortable in his surroundings.

I take the chair beside him. In Hawaiian shirt and bathing suit, I'm just a neighbor taking in some sun. I apply my sunscreen and lean back, steeling myself for the task immediately ahead.

"Mr. Chamberlain?" I ask.

"That's right," he says. "Nate. And who might you be?"

"Name's Dan. Dan Pengar. Ring any bells?" A thousand adolescent indignities flood my head with malice; sacrifice would be too good for the likes of him.

"Sorry, not a one. Where do I know you from?"

This surprises me. I'm lost among the bullied hundreds upon whom he practiced his particular brand of mental and physical cruelties. And here I was certain he'd remember.

"That's not important. Can I have a few minutes of your time -- I have a proposal for you."

"Is this some insurance pitch or something?"

"Not quite. Something of far greater importance."

"I'm not really in much mood for anything serious. I came here just to chill and catch some rays."

"It's about 'The Chosen Ones,' Mr. Chamberlain."

"You from the show?"

"No, sir. I'm here to ask you to consider withdrawing from the show."

"Why would I do that? And who the hell are you anyway?"

"I told you. I represent a small organization dedicated to educating people about the more evil and secret aspects of our so-called government. We can provide protection if you choose to walk away from the show."

"Hey, being chosen is a privilege. Why the heck would anyone want to walk away from that?"

"Well, for one thing, because they kill you. You do understand that's part of the deal, don't you?"

"Look. They're offering three months of a life that'll be fuller and richer than most could ever hope for, living in pampered style with one of the world's most beautiful women. There's no shame in that."

"They sacrifice you. Throw you smack dab into the middle of an active volcano."

Chamberlain smiled and pushed his sunglasses down his nose.

"Ever been in the service?"

"No."

"I was. It was no cakewalk. None of that officer crap. I was a low-level grunt, carrying a far too heavy pack, combing hell-hot sands halfway around the world from here. I knew I could've been taken down at any time: suicide bomber, sniper attack, you name it. But that's the reality I signed up for, defending our great nation. You resolve yourself to knowing you could be gone in an instant."

"But that's military service. "The Chosen Ones" is entertainment."

"To me, it's payoff for grunt time I spent over there. A pretty damn sweet deal too."

"Even if it leads to an untimely end?"

"That part doesn't scare me any – and remember, it's a sacrifice for the greater good."

"You actually believe that government bullshit?"

"What part don't you get? Most guys would give their left nut for a chance to be in 'The Chosen Ones.' And besides, what was it, Dan? I'll be a major celebrity. When I'm gone, people will remember me."

"So your life matters so little you let the government have it on the cheap?"

"You're not listening. The government's giving me a rare prize, buddy boy, and when they do, I bet you'll be there right alongside everyone else, glued to the screen, watching."

"I doubt that."

"Funny how you thought I'd change my mind. Looks like you were dead wrong."

It was an ironic choice of words.

"So there's nothing I can do to change your mind?"

"Tell me your best offer."

"A chance to walk away safely, to keep living until you reach a ripe old age."

"No thanks – I'll take the fame, the celebrity, the high life and the beautiful companion."

"Hey, it's your funeral. Literally. And while everyone watches your private fantasy, the government again will have managed to dupe the unsuspecting public – keeping focus far from the real issues, injustices and inequities."

"I think this conversation's over, Dan. Thanks for your concern."

He offered up a firm handshake and, while tempted to challenge him to a "softest punch contest," instead I just walked away. He was stubborn and determined – and knowing the bully he'd been, a part of me still didn't mind his scheduled demise.

This wasn't how it was supposed to go. Then again, it's exactly how this government remains in power. Their stranglehold on an unsuspecting majority remains secure

– conning everyone into buying into the big beneficence. Standards of living traded for souls. It angered my righteous soul. "But what's one more death in the big scheme of things," I thought, "when Chamberlain seems so happy with his limited lease on the good life."

*   *   *   *   *

In a land of contented, well-monitored idiots, it often seems there's no justice. For the record, Alyssa Manitoba also refused our "walk-away-safe" proposition. Turns out "The Chosen Ones" truly had been well-chosen, loyal to their cause celebre. We subversives were discouraged, but one battle lost doesn't decide the whole war. We lick our wounds and move on.

Since then, I've hacked some government sites in subtle ways, rewriting provided information to better reflect the true reality of what's going on. They haven't even noticed yet – and that's a victory for our side.

In the intervening time, "The Chosen Ones" has aired several episodes. Much as I disliked the Chamberlain who made my young life a living hell, I have to admit he seems made for television now. His rough-hewn manner works well with that muscular presence, and petite, sweet Alyssa is the perfect complement to remove any trace of past bully. They make a beautiful couple, even in high definition.

Chamberlain and Manitoba have won the hearts of the nation, falling in love in a compressed life that seems as star-crossed as those ill-fated Capulet and Montague kids of yore.

As I watch the current installment, Nate's being given a powerful massage. He moans in pained pleasure, lying prone on the padded leather table, as they pound his deltoids and karate chop his spine into submission. This is followed by soaking in a tub of clove-scented oils. I realize they're treating him like meat, tenderizing then marinating.

I can't watch it without thinking they're doomed. It pains me to contemplate the nubile innocence that is Alyssa being terminated so soon.

There is ample newspaper coverage, guest appearances at notable sporting and entertainment events, to say nothing of the merchandising (those yellow "Nate is Great!" buttons are everywhere). True to its billing, "The Chosen Ones" is a media phenomenon. The recap of tonight's episode leads off the late news, with almost no coverage of the ongoing bombings overseas. Still, no one seems to care – what they don't know won't hurt them (or so the government would have them believe).

The fantasy world of "The Chosen Ones" is most engaging. It's easy to lose one's self as witness to that relationship in progress. Their problems seem preferable to any the viewers might have in real life. Better to see physical beauty up close and personal, dancing its way around romance and more; best not to consider that it's heading to an ultimate sacrifice. Perhaps this was the best choice for Chamberlain.

I pick up the phone and punch in numbers, following instructions, entering my choice. The $39.95 seems a bit steep, but I'm confident I'll get my money's worth. Consider it the price of research – or an admission I'm perhaps no better or different than the rest of them. When Chamberlain and I had our discussion, I'd scoffed at the notion of me watching. Yet as I get the recorder set for taping, I have to admit Chamberlain was right.

Begin Again
Rebecca Foust

You think
the worst
is over,

that there's
nothing
left

to learn,
disbelieve,
believe,
endure.

You think
yourself inured
to darkpath
worstcase fear.

But when they
find his bike
parked
at the bridge

— he was the
same age
as your son—

you begin
again
to dream

that dream
you thought
was done

of boys
who climb
the spans
and fall

like leaves
or swans.

111

Empathy
Rebecca Foust

[for Dr. Temple Grandin, Autistic Animal Doctor]

When she was little, visiting her
uncle and aunt's ranch, she liked
to get into the cattle press, flick
the lever to squeeze its sides in,

then she began to believe
she had a body, not just
a collection of electrons
repelling each other in space.

She was thought to lack empathy
for sad events, her classmates' tears,
but she noticed the other things
—rocks getting crushed, stars

that were dying. She hated how
cattle herded for slaughter would mill
about moaning, stamping their hooves,
would sometimes stampede

in eyerolling panic; she noticed
how they moved in the stockyards
to soothe themselves—in circles,
like water. She pondered her need

for pattern and order, how swinging
or rocking could calm her, and she
thought of a way to ease that ascension
to abattoir hell. She thought

of a ramp rising in widening circles,
like water. The feedlot execs could see
a PR trend, so they put the ramps in.
But they didn't see much more than

customers feeling sorry for cows,
not what Aquinas saw, that cruelty
to animals diminishes the human.
They did not, like Temple, wear

bovine skin, snort blood and fear,
flick flies with her tail, speak
to her doomed brethren
in Angus and Brahmin.

Instrument
Rebecca Foust

That
bewildered
look in
your eyes,

the hours
spent liberating
School Project
Butterflies,

your
baffled, raging,
muted-coronet
pain; how you

hated rain
but loved
sun, loved
to shout out,

run and climb on
anything—
until they
taught you to sit

on the rug,
dumbed
your shout-singing
tongue,

instructed
you in the art
of staying
unstrung.

Hope
Rebecca Foust

116

I
Mom starting the
New York Times
crossword the day
she moved to hospice,
the Sunday puzzle

II
The measuring tape
my 12-year-old son
keeps in his bedroom

III
Pap buying corn
on the cob
at the roadside farm stand,
his teeth in his pocket

IV
That thing with feathers ED
was talking about, that will
against all odds
go aloft

V
Bill the dog at the door
where there's never
been a bone

VI
Dad going for the
dog track Trifecta
with his last
forty bucks

VII
Ms. Stone smiling
when we sat down
for our parent conference

VIII
heart carbonation;
maybe it's not
an infarction

IX
the exact shade of pink-red
of the bare-branched
flowering quince

117

X
my friend Gerald
finally getting
a girlfriend

XI
spring after nuclear
winter; nucleus
of anything

XII
no third term
and they're not yet
all dead in Iraq

XIII
perhaps the pilot
won't err this time;
perhaps this time
the doctor is wrong.

An Afternoon
Alyson Mead

She never should have slept with the prosthetic limb
salesman, that much was certain. His car smelled like burning
plastic, and they were here because together they didn't have
enough and alone he couldn't afford a room and she hadn't
known him that long anyway, not long enough to bring him to
her place. His unshaven face had grated against her thigh like
bark as his mouth moved toward her opening, the place where
her insides met the outside, and she was surprised he knew
where to find it or had even bothered, as most guys were wont
to stick it in and forget the rest. They made out and groped
in the front seat of his white Cadillac for awhile, his outspread
hand tenaciously gripping one breast, as if he were steering
her toward the back seat and the hanging squadron of arms
and legs that jiggled from side to side when they moved and
even provided him a tidy income when sales were good.

His hair was warm, slightly greasy and sweet smelling as
it lay against her nostrils. His head was turned away from her
to stare at the door handle. She stared at the car's ceiling,
pockmarked with age and stained brown by the cigarettes he
religiously smoked. Incongruous sounds from outside joined
with their grunts until the roar of them seemed to fill the car
completely—the white noise of the ocean, a gypsy woman
offering fortunes, dulcet as a fishwife, children screeching and
fighting, their flip-flops slapping the pavement.

She arched her back and tried to remember what she'd
seen in this man, what magic had obscured her everyday,

fluorescent supermarket vision with something false and clouded and romantic. It was hard to conjure now, beneath his heavy, dumb body.

It was too late now. She was sitting, on her day off, in the Hollywood Family Planning Clinic, staring at the lavender and pink wallpaper and snatches of accent painting that she guessed were supposed to remind her of her own vagina.

After the sex act with the prosthetic limb salesman, she had gone into a taco stand's bathroom to wash herself off. He was waiting outside the counter that smelled like fried rats, running the car, puffing acrid smoke into the air. She imagined his fingers drumming, nervous and impatient, on the vinyl interior.

When she thought about it now, she could not recall what had made her want to do it. After all, she was educated and relatively experienced about sex. She knew about the dangers of sexually transmitted diseases and how easy it was to get pregnant. She'd even had an abortion at twenty-four, the result of a snap decision made in a New York phone booth on her lunch break when the test had come out positive. Her boyfriend had been furious with her for not consulting with him first, for jettisoning his genes so thoughtlessly. But she tried to explain that it wasn't genes they were talking about, but a person. A needful thing that would derail both of their lives.

How the prosthetic limb salesman had managed to get her to that self-destructive a place she'd never know. There were three drinks, she had been counting, and he was attractive in a dark, Spanish way. Maybe it was the way his eyes smoldered at her, or her lack of patience in wanting to learn what he looked like naked. Where he would put his hands, what he would feel like inside her. Other women drew out the sexual dance to absurd and manipulative proportions, but she had never been able to override her senses.

Now she was faced with waiting and the inevitable decision about whether to keep it. What would a child think about having a fake limb salesman for a father? Would that sort of thing bother a child at all? Perhaps not, but she found it creepy.

She tried to flip through a magazine, convincing herself that none of it mattered. She was a modern woman, and these sorts of things happened sometimes, and it was time to be grown up and strong and just get on with it. Men did this sort of thing all the time, right? They were programmed to fuck and run, to sow the seeds and let someone else worry about the harvesting. Or was that her mother talking?

She glanced up. There were two other women in the room besides the round, Mexican receptionist whispering into the phone. One was a slender woman with a mop of curly red hair. She was chatting into a cell phone that looked like it was made from two black credit cards affixed at an obtuse angle. Her face screwed into a contemptuous frown as she laughed into it.

Perhaps she was in her forties, but it was hard to tell beneath the telltale swell of collagen enhanced lips. The woman was sharp and black and sleek, her body confrontationally toned. Her nails were polished glistening peach, cut and filed into little squares like headstones.

The other one was very young, perhaps fourteen or fifteen. She had black hair chopped off where it met the line of her leather jacket. Scarlet slashes ran across her cheeks to the hairline that was beginning to show light brown roots. Her nails were bitten and stained with something purple and her eyes were smeared with two-day old mascara. Beneath that, her gaze was open and soft, only recently beginning to harden.

She was leaning against the wall, tapping an unlit cigarette against her bare leg very fast, *bangbangbangbang*. Her face was bathed in a thin sheen of sweat. Under that was the nascent acne of adolescence, the red scars of recently healed scratches.

The magazine called pulled her attention back. Inside were women who never seemed to menstruate or fuck or endure complications. They lived in these pages, remaining frozen and timeless and fabulous. She slammed it shut. Who read these things anyway?

The receptionist was crossing something out on a clipboard. There were squeaking sounds of rubber soled shoes on the linoleum. She wondered if she would be called next. There would be the undignified trip to the bathroom to urinate into a plastic cup with her name on it, then the interminable waiting for an answer she did not really want to hear.

She hadn't eaten since this time yesterday, when she'd suddenly been overcome with nausea and prematurely ended a phone conversation with a client to run into the bathroom and puke.

The prosthetic limb salesman hadn't called since Tuesday, though she'd seen him twice more since the sex act in the car. He had tried to have her again but she had, deftly she thought, outmaneuvered him. Instead, he'd taken her to a movie and a coffee, nothing more. She was relieved to rediscover some attractive qualities in him. He had made her laugh and, though not quite smart enough to make the children she'd always imagined bearing, could maintain his end of a conversation.

He promised to call this week sometime, and she hadn't told him about her appointment at the clinic, or her most secret of all desires—she actually wanted children and, if she had to, was not above tricking a man to supply the sperm without his knowledge. Single parenthood could be done, she reasoned, with tenacity and credit cards.

The shoes squeaked again, outside the waiting room door, and then the door opened. The light from inside glistened like new snow.

~

I'd been up since five, when Forrest decided I should be the one to go out and get the morning edition. He calls it that because when he was in high school he wore this hat, I forget what they call it, but sometimes you see them in old movies. The reporters are always wearing them, with little cards stuck into the bands. Anyway, he always wanted to be like those guys—kind-hearted on the inside, but living straight ahead.

See Forrest's hard, I mean not hardcore punk—those guys just scare me. It's just that he has this way of being really smart, like he's been in the world, you know? And yet he can be so cute and cuddly when he wants to be, and he takes care of me now. Well, ever since I left that place where me and some kids were staying in this old theater building. Somebody said they were going to wreck it because Starbucks wanted to have a store there or something and I thought, *well at least I won't have to walk far for coffee in the morning*. But then I met Forrest and I'm making lots of money now.

Well, we are. Together.

So I get the morning edition because Forrest wanted to be a newspaper reporter, and the closest he ever came I guess was after he was arrested for pandering once there was this reporter who came down to the police station to see if there was anything worth covering, you know? He talked to Forrest for about ten minutes and thought, like, his case was all set up and, well, I guess he was maybe gonna write about it so the police would be forced to drop the charges or whatever.

But then nothing ever happened, which seems to be the whole theme of my life lately.

It's not like I'm not in love with Forrest completely, because I am. But it's sometimes, when I have to be the one to go out and get the morning edition, Jackie, the guy I see, can get real cranky and wants to grab me like he thinks he can because I'm asking him for something. I mean, I'm gonna pay for it, so get your hands off the merchandise! Then he'll get crazy and threaten to turn me in to the cops or something. So I have to be all nice and sometimes I don't feel so nice at five o'clock in the morning because I'm tired from working all night and I want to take a bath and forget, maybe drink a beer or something, get high.

It's not like everyone isn't doing something that's a little illegal. People cheat on their taxes all the time. Did you know it's illegal to suck someone's dick in Georgia? It's true. Not like I ever got arrested for it or even did that kind of thing when I was there. It was more like dying of boredom. Getting arrested would have been exciting at that point.

When I came back, Forrest was mostly asleep again, and when he saw me he got up to do the stuff, you know? I came in the door and he was looking at me like I was his savior and let me tell you in that minute I loved him like no one else ever would. He was so new and pink like a baby because he'd just gotten up, and there was a minute there where he looked like he loved me, too.

In that minute I saw something, maybe it was because it's morning, and morning has always been my favorite time of day, ever since I was little. My mother would come in to get me from my bed and she was blond, you know, so her hair was light. We had light yellow curtains, too, like her hair but with little holes cut in it. It has a name I can't remember.

In the morning she came in with this yellow hair and yellow curtains, and everything was just so perfect in that one minute, all warm under the covers, like anything that happened that day would be good. I remember that.

Anyway, Forrest looked at me like that, then he started cooking the stuff up. He was all concentrating and thinking hard about the drug, I guess. I asked if I could help, but he just looked at me like he wished I were dead. I mean, I know he didn't mean it because I'd just gotten the morning edition and he always said he would die without the morning edition. So I had kind of saved his life, you know?

I sat on the edge of the bed and watched him doing this thing that happens pretty much every day at the same time and then again at night. He started to do it, you know? Just touched the beginning of the vein outside the skin and I felt something, I mean I wanted to, I don't know. I put my hand on his shoulder very lightly, just so. Then his eyes hated me again and he hit me with the backside of his hand.

I fell back on the bed and touched my jaw. I could never believe Forrest would do that, because he was always so nice. I mean, once in awhile he belted me, when I mouthed off or something, but he always said he would teach me things. So I guess this was one of my lessons.

He finished what he was doing and then his arm just gave out and relaxed on the bed there. I saw the needle in his hand, and his fingers loosen. His eyes were almost closed. I took the needle out of his hand because I wanted to share it with him, to see why Forrest loved it more than me. There was a little left in the tip of the thing so I tapped it with my finger like I'd seen him do and then pushed the needle into a big, honkin' vein that was standing about a foot off the back of my hand. I held it there all stiff on the leg of my jeans until I could make the needle work. All the rest of it went into me the way I wished I could hold him inside, like a big gulp of air.

There was a little pain in my hand, like when they take blood, but I was used to that. I started to feel dizzy and strange and then I hoped Forrest hadn't seen what I had done. I put the needle on the table, where he could see it.

Then I felt real sick all of a sudden and grabbed my stomach through my shirt. I remembered the guy Forrest made me go with last night and the way his face got all scrunched up and angry, like he was mad at me, when I was just laying there like I was supposed to. His dick was wrinkled and angry like he was and there were little hate lines around his lips that had been dug in from years of this, I guess.

I held onto my stomach with one hand and covered my mouth with the other so I didn't throw up on the floor, because last time when I had the flu Forrest made me clean up twice after I threw up by mistake.

I almost made it. Just a little went on the floor and then I was crouched over the toilet and praying. I remembered the prayer my mom had taught me, the one I spoke inside my head on the way to kindergarten when I had to walk past the black girls I was convinced were plotting to beat me up, the one I said in my head when my father appeared in my dream after he was long dead and said I was a no good slut. I said it in my head all the next day when I woke up and it still didn't help. I had to drink four scotches to get to work in one piece. I saw the baby that was probably inside me. He came into my head suddenly, like a bullet of cuddly flesh, and I was afraid.

Who would he look like?

I got Veronica to drive me to the clinic and they took one look at me and my hair I guess. I have this black hair that Forrest made me get because he said I looked like the Black Dahlia. She was a girl in L.A. who got killed and everyone was in love with her so I thought that was cool, and when I started reading about her life, I thought maybe I could be the reincarnation of her now. Forrest says I'm tragic just like she was. I know he really loves me.

124

Then they started asking all these personal questions like *where did you get those bruises* and *have you had any unprotected sex lately* and *do you have health insurance.* Like I'm going to have health insurance. I don't even pay taxes, lady.

I filled out the forms they had, but it seemed like a lot of work and I wondered when I could see a doctor. I didn't need the third degree. Not like I fuckin' did anything.

There was this real prissy bitch sitting there in a black suit. Old thing, too, wearing bell-bottoms. Like they didn't go out with the seventies. She was looking at me like I had some kind of disease and talking on the phone the whole time like she was Miss Importance. Well, I thought, I can talk on the phone, too. So I went over to the pay phone to see if I could track down Forrest. He must be worried sick about me. I didn't even tell him where I'd gone and he wouldn't be able to find me after my eleven o'clock.

A nice lady in a white jacket came out and asked me if I'd ever had an HIV test. I told her I read the papers, and she didn't need to pussyfoot around me. She said they'd need some blood and I thought *get in line behind everyone else.*

~

The nurse practitioner had managed to get the cell phone out of her hand by the time they got inside the examination room. Then she asked the flame-haired woman to disrobe and put on a paper gown, closing the door behind her.

Dutifully, the flame-haired woman lay back on the leatherette examination table, stiff as a winter clothesline. She put the phone beside her right ear and looked at the ceiling.

She thought of clouds.

There were clouds before, she remembered that much. There was sky, too, during her Los Angeles childhood, herself the child of movie actors and no stranger to privilege. There were late night swimming pools smelling sweet as teenage sweat and huge, buttery moons and definitely clouds, before the dark had taken them.

The door opened with a click that made her shiver up to her neck. The nurse practitioner asked a few half-hearted questions about her studio job, if she'd read the literature about mammographies from her last visit.

The flame-haired woman grunted a non-committal response. There was no way this ill-tailored bitch was going to tell her what to do in her three minutes of discretionary time each week, between the workouts, the facials, body waxing, not to mention the electrolysis of every arm and leg hair, the pain of which required numbing cream she wore under Saran Wrap in the office, frightening her assistants when they came in to find her trussed like leftovers and listening to submission tapes. The only reason she was at this damn clinic in the first place was because it was the studio head's favorite charity, and she'd promised to help out. Now at least she could say she'd been there.

There was the pressure again behind her eyes, from the job, itself not worth the three hundred or so grand it paid her each year, plus royalties on the soundtrack albums that did anything on the charts. The constant parties, the premieres, the non-stop parade of much younger men more than willing to bounce her, almost old enough to be their grandmother, on their knees.

125

The nurse fussed with instruments, then gently separated her legs. *Relax,* she said. A palm flattened against her aerobicized stomach. The flame-haired woman fought a deep groan that wanted to come out.

A black music star had liked to visit her for a time, before he'd hooked up with Vanessa Williams' sister or cousin or something. She'd served him popcorn and champagne and made sure to bend over in front of him as much as possible. Sometimes he ruined her expensive clothes when he tore them off. She liked it when he held her down by the neck, pressing her face into the whiteness of the pillowcase so hard she left bright lipstick smears.

When he left her alone in the echoing chambers of her house, there was always the phone to keep her company. One time she beeped an assistant at eleven thirty on a Saturday night to bitch him out about not sending her home with the right phone sheet, but instead a truncated version no doubt designed to ruin her career and destroy her reputation. He apologized and said he would go into the office first thing the next morning, print out a new one and fax it to her at home. But she'd insisted, working herself into a redfaced frenzy, that he get up to the studio right then, now in fact, and send it to her.

Some people only understood when you yelled.

Confrontation builds character—that's what her father had always said. She'd started out wanting to be an actress like her mother and had failed miserably at auditions, every vibrant molecule of her shrinking and dying in front of the casting agents. Her father had given her nightly lectures on the value of confrontation, and made her repeat her sides into the mirror until her eyes were puffy and her voice hoarse.

Her father had also made her hold cans of soup with her arms outspread to build strength. *Nothing worse than hanging flesh on a woman,* he said.

She had her first plastic surgery at fourteen, a rhinoplasty gift from her mother at her first menstruation. She was a late bloomer and anxious to initiate herself into the ways of the world. Boys, then men, saw her as small and insufficient, and she was content to let it stay like that as long as she'd be taken care of, if she'd be loved and paid for and pampered.

The nurse pushed what looked like a circular prism inside her and scowled.

The flame-haired woman thought of the sixty or so calls that would be itemized on her desk when she got back, the round of meetings for which she spent every minute preparing yet rarely felt prepared for. She thought of the enormous pile of unopened CDs on her bedroom floor, next to the twenty thousand dollar stereo system she never had time to play.

She felt pressure inside her, and a vast aloneness inside her heart.

The white-coated woman looked up from the microscope and asked if she'd had any pain.

She was afraid to tell her about the last time she'd had sex, about the bleeding that went on for days. Rather than allow the maid this ruddy personal detail, she'd stuffed the ruined sheets into an oversized gym bag, then disposed of them in the locker room garbage can.

There was safety in a negative answer. She shook her head and darted a glance at the phone next to her ear. Comfort welled in her.

The nurse kept frowning. There were some irregular cells in her last pap smear, she reminded.

Her father was sitting home even now, riddled with cancer, mutating cells spreading from his throat through his lungs and into his lymph system. He raged against it until they hired a twenty-four hour nurse and bodyguard. Sometimes, they found him cursing and making fists at the moon, alone in the garden, or tearing the rare, imported plants from the earth by their stems.

He called *The Hollywood Reporter* and pretended to be his own press agent, giving news of his impending comeback film with Kirk Douglas as his co-star and Billy Wilder attached to direct. Anita Loos was to write the screenplay, and they were talking to Gloria Swanson about playing the ingenue. He drank endless cups of coffee, spilling them on his boxer shorts and remaining wild-eyed into the night.

She imagined herself eaten up from inside and wanted to laugh, after all the work she'd done—the surgery, the fucking maintenance. She imagined herself old and shrunken and stealing withered heads of cabbage from the Mayfair Market, growing frailer in the length of days. She imagined the embarrassment of incontinence and having her cell phone taken away from her. She wanted to laugh.

An urge to wolf chocolate came over her, then disappeared just as quickly as it had come. Calmness descended.

She would put on the sleek black clothing and pay her bill, then make her way out to her equally sleek car. She would pass those two other girls, less fortunate than herself. Maybe she would go to the gym early today.

She would pretend not to wait for the results of her tests.

She sat up, holding the tattered remains of the paper gown to her breastbone. The cell phone fit perfectly in her hand.

Her gaze was pulled to her watch. She had to go. After all, she couldn't stay here all day. It was still afternoon, and there were so many calls to return.

After Tilling
Barb Lundy

In the spring, his touch stirred what
she could not reach alone. His breath
paced the interspace of her sleep.

He seeded squash and sweet peas in dry
soil mixed with loam. She harrowed the
north edge, planted artichokes.

Their words puddled in the
humidity of August. Stagnated
to spare exchange.

In half-light they steam a harvest
flower of green blades. She rips
a leaf and pulls it between her teeth.

They dip petal edge pulp in warm butter.
Tear until one heart lies between them.
Her blade slices its tender flesh in two.

For the Love of Pearl
Rob Lavender

Jim Gosling fell in love with Pearl—a pole dancer at the Shamrock Lounge—who was born with a scanner between her legs that broadcast crime from across America. As she danced and broadcast crimes, it sent different impulses through Jim's body. What he felt during a breaking and entering was unlike what he experienced during domestic violence. An armed robbery or murder became so intense Jim would shudder at his table. He couldn't explain it. No one could. And sometimes during her show, when the audience was still, Jim could smell gunpowder and taste a metallic grit when she broadcast a drive-by shooting. There would be the sound of tires squealing, of shots being fired, of screams, and then complete silence until she picked up the frequency of a new crime. Some fainted, landing face first into the wood floor of the Shamrock Lounge, while protesters circled the building, screaming, "Get that demon out of our town!"

At first Jim didn't know what to make of all of this. He believed Pearl's scanner might be a carnival trick. Maybe she had something hidden inside her bikini. Maybe it was an illusion. Maybe it was the real thing. He wasn't sure. But she mesmerized him. Even law enforcement flocked to Leper's Fork to hold their conventions. They'd wolf-whistle and yell, "We'll get their asses. Don't you worry, Pearl." She renewed their passion for justice and lowered the stress of their profession.

When law enforcement officers returned home and responded to crimes, they imagined Pearl. They remembered the way she danced with greater velocity when a high-speed chase ensued or how she banged the scanner against the pole when the scanner broadcast a murder. They remembered the look on her face as if she was the one dying instead of their victim.

Some believed Pearl's condition was due to some kind of genetic screw up. Pearl's mother believed her daughter's extraordinary gift was due to lonely days she spent dispatching at the police station while pregnant with Pearl. This was back when her husband was the chief of police in Leper's Fork. Back before he died in the line of duty. No one knew for sure where the scanner originated. Some questioned its authenticity. But Jim didn't care about the scanner's origin. He believed she was God's gift to a dysfunctional nation and couldn't get his mind off what the bikini concealed. He wanted to see it. Maybe touch it. Put his ear to the speaker. Get a closer look. *Was the scanner a black box? Did it have a grille covering a speaker?*

Jim had five Piggly-Wiggly brand spiral notebooks filled with sketches of Pearl. Sometimes Jim drew the crime as she broadcast it. He drew masked gunmen shooting bullets at the audience. He drew rappers being gunned down. He sketched a serial killer's latest victim. Drew the victim lying face down in the inner city. Sometimes face up with harrowing eyes. If the scanner reported domestic violence, he drew an exploding house after rockets shaped as fists slammed into it. But some nights when he felt sensual he'd sketch Pearl without the bikini that concealed the scanner's identity. On Saturdays he tricked it out with violent florescent lights circling the scanner like fluid. He put a different grille on it each Sunday. He drew a cross in the middle and draped a chain over it with a padlock. Then he'd draw a veil over Pearl's face and a halo of light above her head. But he wanted more than his sketches offered, and he hated and never understood why conservative Christians called Pearl demonic, even though they loved the money she generated with her shows in Leper's Fork. These people infuriated him so much that he even had a T-shirt airbrushed that read, "Don't Trample My Pearl You Bunch of Pigs." They egged his truck on numerous occasions.

One hot August day, the Shamrock's air-conditioning unit stopped working. It happened during Pearl's first act. While the out-of-town law enforcement men drank and whistled, Pearl sweat so much the scanner short-circuited and sparks shot out of her bikini. Then sirens blasted. Blue lights flashed. Shots were fired and doughnuts commenced to flying out, rolling onto the Shamrock's floor. This was when Jim charged the stage and tackled Pearl, as the law enforcement agents drew their guns. Moments later Paul, the Shamrock's owner, was helping Jim hold her down. She was shaking.

Jim wasn't sure what to say or do. A bouncer tried to rip him away from her, but Paul made the bouncer stop.

"It's okay," Paul told the bouncer. "Just close the place down."

"The shows are cancelled until further notice," the bouncer yelled. He had his arms fanned out, sweeping the crowd toward the exit while some booed.

Paul told Jim, "Let's get her up and sit her down over there at the table, and I'll call her momma to come and get her."

"I can take her home," Jim said.

"No, that's not necessary. Just sit her down over there. I'll be right back."

Jim sat her at his table and took a closer look at her facial features. He'd never been this close before.

Paul returned from behind the bar.

"Pearl, your momma's line is busy. Probably on the computer. So just sit tight until I get through to her," Paul said, leaning down looking into Pearl's eyes. "You still look dizzy. I'm just glad that damn siren stopped."

"What happened?" Jim asked.

"She got too hot. That's all. She'll be fine."

"I can take her home," Jim said. "Where does she live?"

"Her momma would kill me. Pearl isn't allowed to ride with anyone but her, so can't ruffle her feathers, if you know what I mean. Woman can chew a hole in your ass."

"Okay," Jim said. "But if she stays in here, she's gonna get hot again. At least let me take her to my truck and put her in the air-condition."

"Yeah, you probably right. Let's take her on out of here..." My nerves can't take that shit again. Go pull your truck around back. My damn jalopy ain't got no air."

"Pearl," Paul said. "We gonna take you outside and put you in Jim's truck. It's too hot in here."

Jim hustled to the parking lot where law enforcement men were cussing and laughing at what had transpired with Pearl. Jim thought, *I ought to kill the pig bastards.* He hopped in his truck and peeled out in the gravel. The tires threw rocks against the Shamrock's metal building. He hoped one would ricochet and hit them.

Paul and Pearl met him at the backdoor. They put her in the truck.

"I'm gonna go back in and try her momma again."

"We'll get you cooled down," he told Pearl.

She offered a weak smile. He shut the passenger door and rounded the truck. He got behind the wheel.

"My name is Jim, by the way."

"Thanks for helping me," she whispered.

Jim couldn't believe it. For almost a year, he'd had the impression she was a deaf-mute.

"Tell me where you live, and I'll take you home."

Pearl gave him a funny look.

"I swear I'll take you right home. No funny business. I'm sure you want to get home so you can lie down, don't you?"

"Sure, why not. Momma's just gonna raise hell with me all the way home. Tell me how I should've known better than dancing in that kind of heat. But it didn't seem that hot. And please don't tell anyone I spoke to you."

"You ever, uh, short-circuited before or whatever that was that happened in there."

"Oncet," she said.

Jim saw Paul approaching the truck and put the truck in gear. "Just tell me the directions. Do I turn left or right out of the parking lot?"

She sat up in the bench seat, looked both ways, and said, "Left."

Jim let out on the clutch, mashed the gas pedal, and spun the wheels in a mud puddle. Then the tires caught the pavement and barked like a seal. He got the truck up to speed as mud slapped the underside of the truck, and then flew straight up in the air, spreading out in all directions on the highway. The highway moaned beneath the mud tires while tobacco fields, auburn in the sunset, waxed and waned in the side window of the truck. The long antenna mounted at the rear of the cab was in a sword fight with an invisible foe, and Jim checked his rearview mirror.

"You know where Tinker Diary Farm is down here on the right?" Pearl asked.

"Yeah."

"Take a right by it. That's Brown Road. I live about sixteen miles up on the left."

"I didn't know the road went that far back in there."

Her scanner started working again. But instead of a crime, it broadcast a police officer reciting the Miranda Rights to a criminal.

"Hang on, let me turn it down. I can't hear you over top of this damn scanner." Pearl reached under her bikini and fiddled with something. "Oaky, what did you say?"

Jim sat there stunned. All this time, and he'd never thought to draw a volume control knob. He realized there was a lot he didn't know about Pearl.

"Nothing," Jim said. "I got it. Turn on Brown Road."

Pearl smiled and reached over to turn up the radio. "I like this song," she said. "Everybody told me you were a deaf-mute."

"I know. Everybody thinks I am. It makes it easier on my momma, especially after I was on Oprah. This way people aren't driving her or me crazy with questions. But it ain't easy having to stay quiet while this damn scanner broadcasts doom and gloom all night."

"You been on *Oprah?*"

"Yeah."

"You've been on *The Oprah Winfrey Show?*"

"Momma said she'd never go on there again. She got mad when Oprah wanted me to go put on a bikini and walk out in front of God and everybody. Momma didn't think the world had a right to see or hear my gift. She told Oprah that my gift ain't available for public consumption. That's just the way she said it too. Momma said we were there because we hoped someone watching would have a cure. Then Oprah said, 'Well, you gotta let us at least hear it . . . Right?'She extended her arm to her audience as if she had the power to change my momma's mind. But Oprah don't know my momma."

"That makes sense, but why are you dancing at the Shamrock?"

"For the money. I'm trying to buy my own place so I won't have to live with Momma the rest of my life. Plus, I got the idea from Oprah. After she asked me to put on a bikini and come out for her audience, I thought, *That's how I'll make my living one day.*"

Pearl lunged for the dial on the radio and said, "This is a great station." Pearl started singing along with the song on the radio.

Jim smiled and was content to let her enjoy the music. He didn't want to ask too many questions.

Brown Road was nothing but miles and miles of trees bending and twisting along a gravel road. The truck shot a rooster tail of dust behind it while Jim watched her every move. He watched the way the trees cast different shades of light on her face as they passed beneath them. He noticed how she widened her eyes, grabbed her stomach and giggled when Jim gunned the truck over a rise in the road. He loved the way she screamed and grabbed the dashboard when they plunged through a creek bed without slowing down. Jim liked hearing her laugh. He didn't want the adventure to end.

During a commercial break on the radio, Jim said, "You look like you're feeling better."

"Yeah. It was just too hot in there."

"You were working pretty hard."

She only smiled.

"Not that you don't on other nights."

"Momma won't let me listen to rap," she said, changing the subject.

"Yeah? Why?"

"She says it might make me wanna marry a rapper."

They both laughed.

"You ever been married?" Jim asked.

"Oncet."

"Yeah?"

"Yeah." A smile grew across her face. He liked making her smile. He slid down in his seat and tapped out the beat of the country song on the steering wheel.

"How 'bout you? You ever been hitched?"

"Nope."

"Really? And how old are you?"

"Old enough to know better and young enough to do it."

"You're funny, Jim."

Jim chuckled.

"How long were you married?"

"About a year. He was a mean bastard."

"Did you kill him?"

"He needed killin'. Said I was a freak radio. Said his momma was right about me. Said a woman that can't procreate needs a stake in the heart. He eventually gave me one and dropped me off at my momma's house."

"The bastard."

Pearl laughed.

Jim was driving in the middle of the road, looking at Pearl when suddenly they met a car in the bend of a curve. He swerved when Pearl screamed and put her hands on the dashboard. He missed the oncoming car, but the car ran off the road and landed in a gulley.

Jim stopped the truck, and they both looked back through the rear windshield.

"That's just my luck," Pearl said.

Jim looked at her and said, "Wasn't your fault."

"That's Momma. Bet she was coming after me."

"You've got to be kidding?"

"Nope. Don't you dare tell her I talked to you."

"Get down in the seat and stay in the truck. I'll get her out, and then we'll beat her back to the Shamrock."

Jim opened the door and jumped out. He ran to her momma's car, leaning on its side in the gulley. Betty, her momma, had fired the engine and was trying to get the car out, but the tires kept spinning in the red clay. When Jim tapped on the window, she cut the engine and tried to open the door.

Jim helped her get it open, and then said, "You all right?"

"You crazy fool. Look what you done made me do. Don't just stand there. Grab my hand and help me out."

Jim took both her hands inside his large ones, pulled her out, and steadied her in the gravel road.

"Mister, you can't drive this road like a bat out of hell. Don't you know it dead ends up there? Who in the hell are you? Never seen you on this road before."

"My name is Jim Gosling. I live over on the old Steed farm."

"You that ex-priest, ain't you?"

"I guess you can say that. I like to think I'm a farmer now."

"Well, get out your colored beads or whatever you bunch of Catholics use in prayer, because my car best not have a scratch on it."

Pearl hopped out of the truck and walked up to where they stood, revealing herself.

"Pearl, what in tar-nation are you doing with this fool? You all right? Paul called and said you'd had another one of your fainting spells. Don't say nothing." She stuck her hand out like a traffic cop. "Walk over here and let me see you."

Betty led Pearl to the front of Jim's truck.

"Hey," Jim called after them. "I'm gonna see if I can get your car out."

They never responded, so Jim climbed inside the leaning car and fired the engine. He revved it and dumped the clutch, but it only spun the wheels. He tried it repeatedly, but cut the engine when smoke boiled from beneath the hood.

"Hey, Pearl?"

Jim could see them talking, but couldn't hear what they were saying.

"Hey, lady?" he yelled louder.

Betty said, "We a-coming. Hold your taters."

When they walked back to the car, Jim said, "It won't budge. But I got a rope in my truck. Let me see if I can pull it out. If I can't you'll have to call a wrecker."

"You best get it out, because you'll be the one calling and paying for the wrecker."

Jim freed the car on his second attempt with Betty behind the wheel.

Jim captured the moment of that day in his next sketch. He drew her beside him in the seat of his truck. Her hair flowed across the passenger side and out the window, and then down the side of the truck. He colored his truck red, even though it was black. And the smile was the centerpiece of the drawing. But when he showed it to Pearl the following week at the Shamrock Lounge, she took his colored pencil, put an X over her mouth, and stomped off, puzzling Jim.

Jim called after her, but she didn't respond. She took the stage and danced while a crime took place somewhere in the Heartland.

For a solid month, Jim ran the scenario over in his mind, but could not figure out what he'd done to offend her. Then one Friday, he decided to stay away. He watched television, but couldn't get interested in any program for wondering what Pearl's scanner was broadcasting down at the Shamrock Lounge.

Then the next day in the evening redness, Betty knocked on Jim's door. He'd taken what was going to be a short afternoon nap, but suddenly realized he'd been asleep for three hours. He peeped through the diamond-shaped window in the door and discovered Betty on his front porch.

"Open up, Jim Gosling. You hear me? Open this damn door."

By the time he undid the three latches and unbolted the deadbolt, her patience had run out.

"Where is she you little pervert? I know what y'all do with God's children. I know you got her. Get out of my way." Betty pushed Jim aside and entered. "Pearl! You better get your ass out here. Don't play this shit with me. I'll send you back to the institution."

Jim said, "Betty, Pearl is not here."

Betty searched every room while Jim followed. No Pearl. Then she fell apart and couldn't say shit with a mouthful of words. All she could do was blubber.

"Calm down," Jim told her. "Take you a breath."

She did.

Then she said, "Somebody done took Pearl. I thought you had her. I guess I hoped you had her. You don't have her, do you?"

"Shit!" Jim said. "I knew that was gonna happen."

"Can you help me find her? We have to find her?"

"You called the police?"

"Yeah. They have boys patrolling for her. But I figured I'd help. Probably cover more ground than those knot-heads. Plus, I won't rest a minute until we find her."

"Let me drive you."

"Well, that's not a bad idea. I can't see good at night."

"Let me get my keys."

Jim immediately blamed himself. He should've been watching Pearl as God had commissioned him. He thought about kneeling and praying, but stopped himself.

Betty had her hand on the door handle of Jim's truck when he came back from retrieving the keys.

"We'll find her," Jim said, as they climbed inside the truck.

"Hurry," she said.

Jim cranked the truck and headed down the driveway so fast all the cows looked up. He turned onto the highway and headed east. He didn't know why. He just had this gut feeling that everything evil must turn left, and they traveled into the hazy vaporization that was there one minute and gone the next.

Betty said, "If you're not found in the first 48 hours, you're probably dead."

"Is that what the police said?"

She didn't answer.

"You think those out-of-town policemen took her?"

Betty didn't answer. She had the same glaze over her eyes that Jim had noticed over Pearl's.

Jim looked over at Betty, as he slumped over the wheel sucking at his teeth, and said, "Betty, do you think her dancing is demonic? Do you think we should make her stop?"

Betty stared straight-ahead. She never turned to acknowledge his question.

"Well, you don't have to talk. We'll find her. Don't worry."

Betty leaned out the truck window and yelled, "Pearl!" into every crevice in Leper's Fork while Jim drove at half-speed. They crept along like a farmer inspecting his crop, fearful that nightfall would bring more mystery. By 3AM, nothing had emerged. They searched every inch of the county. They thought about searching the whole state of Tennessee, but decided to get a fresh start the next day.

Floodlights on the trailer automatically came on when Betty and Jim parked. Jim got out and stood with slouched shoulders and his hands in his pockets while Betty searched for her key.

She opened the door, turned back toward Jim, and said, "Thank you, Jim."

"We're not giving up. You hear me? We'll find her."

She only shook her head and walked inside.

After Jim let Betty out, he continued to search for Pearl. He didn't sleep for two days. He burnt three tanks of gas.

Had beef jerky for breakfast, lunch, and dinner. It left a bad taste in his mouth.

Two weeks after Pearl's disappearance, the phone rang.

"We found her, Jim. She's in Nashville. She's okay."

"Thank God," Jim said. "Do we need to go get her?"

"No, the boys down at the police department that knew her dad are on their way to get her."

"How did she wind up in Nashville?"

"One of them Kilpatrick boys from Johnson Hollow took her and left her at a truck stop."

"Did he kidnap her?"

"No, she got in the car with him after one of her shows. Evidently, they met when she was sixteen at the psych hospital after Pearl short-circuited the first time."

"Really," Jim said, thinking about the sweating incident at the Shamrock.

"Jim, I think Pearl is in love with him. She wants to go live with him in Johnson Hollow. What should I do? I told her a man that loves you don't leave you at a truck stop."

"I know that's right."

Jim felt his face flush. He couldn't believe his reaction to the news that Pearl loved someone and wanted to move. Maybe it was because he'd pictured himself rescuing her. He'd pictured her beside him in the truck again, and he wanted to kill the Kilpatrick boy.

Betty said, "I don't know why she ain't mentioned that boy before. Evidently, he promised her he'd come get her when he got out of the psych hospital."

"Well, I'll be damned. I guess he made good on his promise," Jim said.

"Jim?"

"Yeah."

Jim waited, but her words didn't come.

"I'm here."

"Jim, she ain't right. The boy done messed her up."

"What do you mean, 'not right'? Did he bust her up? Bruise her?" Then Jim said what he almost couldn't say, "Did he rape her?"

"Worse than that."

Jim was thinking, *What can be worse than that?*

"She ain't normal. I don't know how to explain it."

"Should I come over?"

"No, I don't want anyone to see her like this, especially not you, Jim. You've been so good to help me."

The only thing Jim could think to say next was, "Did you know that Kilpatrick boy is an inbred?" He wasn't sure why he'd said it.

"I have to go, Jim."

"Please call me later. Let me know how she's doing."

Jim ran the conversation through his mind repeatedly. He guessed Pearl liked hearing romantic gestures from that inbred. Alls she ever heard was doom and gloom, so maybe she was happy to hear the words, "I think I love you," even if they came from the mouth of an inbred. Jim wasn't sure.

When detectives interrogated the Kilpatrick boy, he denied any feelings of love for Pearl. After a grueling interrogation, the deputies came for a beer at the Shamrock and told the story while Jim sat and listened. The inbred boy said Pearl was part of his mission to crack the code of a combination lock on a storage unit that contained the Third Throne of the Holy Trinity. He thought making love to Pearl might heighten or decipher some of the police codes he thought he'd heard from her scanner when they were at the psych hospital. But no one else has ever heard her broadcast police codes, only crime. At that time, he'd written the police codes down, but he wasn't able to crack the code of the combination lock with them. So he came back for more codes. And together the inbred and Pearl built a love shack out of boxes by the river. He made love to Pearl, but no one was quite sure how it happened. He said he'd never experienced anything like it. Their bodies going at it while she jabbered out crimes. It was the high-speed chase with sirens blasting that finally got him, he said.

He told detectives, "I made her feel like a woman. You can't fault a man for that."

The one thing he was guilty of was trying to tune Pearl's scanner with a screwdriver. He wanted to hear police codes from different planets. But he somehow changed the frequency of Pearl's scanner and tuned it to truck drivers instead.

The Kilpatrick boy said Pearl liked hearing truckers talking about a trucker's life. She told him, "It sounds so different from crimes."

He told them, "How was I supposed to know making a woman out of her would make her love a trucker's life?"

The inbred said Pearl liked hearing the roar of their motors as they keyed the mikes on their CBs. She listened all night, the first night. Didn't sleep. Listened all day the next day. Then all night the next night. Didn't sleep for three days. Not one wink. She wanted to hear them cuss and tell nasty jokes. A few talked about Christ. They explained why they had big crosses lit up on the fronts of their trucks. Soon she wanted to see where the truckers ate, where they pissed, where they showered. That's why she talked the inbred into taking her to a truck stop.

After hanging out for a few days at the truck stop and after Pearl had ridden in ten semis, the boy got anxious. He wanted to try his luck with the new police codes he'd memorized while making love to Pearl. But Pearl wouldn't leave, so he left without her.

When the good people of Limestone County heard that Pearl no longer broadcast crime, the conservative Christians said she deserved every nasty truck driver on the road.

They were glad her crime fantasies were over. They thanked God for his intervention—never realizing their prayers were producing a lower clientele. Meaner men and nasty hecklers were the fruits of their laboring prayers. And Jim said they got what they deserved—a new truck stop beside the Shamrock Lounge. But Jim couldn't watch her dance any longer. Her trucker frequency broadcast steamy trucker talk and the whereabouts of radar enforcement while she danced. He couldn't stomach it. Could not enjoy one moment of it. So he sat in the Shamrock and tried to sketch her from memory, but usually wound up getting mad at the inbred. If only that inbred hadn't damaged her and made her the maladjusted one, then he'd have new sketches for his Piggly-Wiggly spiral notebook. But Jim couldn't sketch or think romantically about the scanner between her legs anymore. His imagination only produced crude questions that made him feel deeper regret. *Where did the Kilpatrick boy stick the screwdriver? Did she wrap her legs around him when they made love? How did it feel to make love to her while she broadcast a high-speed chase? Did she reach down and turn the volume up on the scanner? Would he ever know? Did he ever want to know?*

Smoke
Kyla Hanington

There was a man on a bike
And a man not on a bike
And they passed by the broken window of the dance club.
The window was black.
It was one o'clock in the morning.
Farhenheit 36 degrees.
Of course all the windows were black,
So no one could see the people dancing.

And I walked with Tom, my imaginary lover.
And that was when I was still in love
with his hands,
And the way he smelled like smoke,
And the scar of a dog bite worn like
a battle-wound upon his thigh.
And I imagined a house
with pig-coloured steps that led to the lawn.
And that would be Tom's house.
And it would be big and comfortable.
Just like Tom.
And my apartment would be cluttered and empty.
Just like me.

And we passed.
Tom and I,
and the man on the bike,
and the man not on the bike.

And we said "hello".
And our breath was like smoke.
Each of us,
breathing smoke to the other.

Sad Sad Road
Kyla Hanington

Through the trees Clara spotted the turn
to Sad Sad Road
along which Joe McCloskey
lived for a while with another man's wife.

They went camping, ate hot dogs, dropped
crab traps off the Neck Point rocks. Having
never done such things, she
mocked him in imagined conversations
with friends she no longer had.

Did he know? He swept the beer cans
from the cab of his truck and one afternoon
replaced the cougar picture in the living
room with a purple starfish made from clay.

What attempts at house-keeping were these?
Surely he could never woo her, she knew as
she watched him from his old brown couch.

From Joe's house you can see the ocean
You can see the drop off where she dropped off.

After even this man, 145 pounds of sinew,
fawn goatee, last date
a fat girl from the internet,
even this man in the end
moved on.

Upon The Lost
Daniel Buckwalter

I slept with Mary for three years. She shouts that it was five years, but I say we broke up three times — at least — for two years. She counters that we are always connected in thought. That is testament to Mary's Top Forty outlook on life, the rhyming verses and sloganeering choruses. It's sick because she's right. We were each other's pacifier. We suckled poison from the other's dysfunction, fueled at the start line every night by alcohol and extended by any drugs that were handy. Even now, we argue about the length of our tortured romance and its nuances the way historians debate wars gone by. We have theories and opinions, then declare Hail to the Victors and watch two minds disintegrate.

It's not as if we lived together, though it did seem that way. I have my small home, and Mary bounced around four apartments that I can recall. But we needed each other, and we deserved each other. Those early dreams after college of success by public deed were rolling clouds without lightning spines, wishes that could not be fulfilled. We talked of great matters, but we independently understood that we were more afraid of the heights we longed for than the basement of emotional development where we lived. So long as we were tangled in our mutual distress calls — and the sex was good — we could keep the wolves at bay. We wanted to speak personally, I'm sure. I wanted to. I wanted to say I love you to Mary in quiet tones, to be stationary and talk of non-sensical topics, to laugh at the day. Instead, there were first-call drinks, dinner out — we always went out to "do something" — then drunken wine to top off the night. Weeks and months became a blurry three years of silent physical demolition, and the silence left the ground free for weedy emotional resentments. There were the finer, trivial things, of course, and there were the weighty issues. The biggest was that I never met her parents. To this day I have not met them. They don't know I exist. To her parents, Mary was hopelessly single and out of date, and to Mary, I guess, I was a mortifying phase of her life, to be kept under lock and key.

The journey must have looked like two jalopies colliding in an endless crazy-eight loop, but its end came at the beginning. I know that now. For the record, the white flag dropped in September, two long years ago. It was a bitter, profanity laced two-way tirade with each of us shredding the other's humanity. I almost hit her. It was the only time I came close to that. Mary screamed abstract thoughts: "We have nothing in common ... It's all about the fuck with you ... God dammit, Joey, I hate you. Get out!" She moved into a home with another woman. I heard second-hand that she dated three men before playing house with a man who was mean, controlling and alcoholic. A friend told me that one night, at the restaurant he worked at, Mary and her man devolved into an arguing, drunken couple and were kicked out. And that would be the last I would hear of her, I thought. I went into rehab for sixty days, paid for by my parents. I discovered meetings and feelings, steps and traditions, early nights and earlier mornings. At some point, no matter the crossroads, you are who you are in cement shoes. Nothing, not even alcoholic recovery, can fundamentally alter your DNA. When I asked a counselor, late in the sixty-day confinement, how sick he believed I was, he laughed. "You just stay with us for the rest of your life." So I am trying to mend the frayed edges and be a presentable man. I am trying to develop new habits and outlooks, and even pull the shades apart to let the sun pierce through. I have taken up running and cycling in an attempt to get in shape. My life seems narrower, less cluttered with the baggage of others. I haven't felt this good since high school.

Which made the phone call this morning such a jolt. It was Mary, it was 8 o'clock, painfully early for a Saturday morning, and it confused me. She had to repeat twice that it was her, and after that, I was in tune with her girlish voice, even at age 30, though it seemed hesitant, as if she wasn't sure this was a good idea. Hell, I wasn't sure this was a good idea, but it had been two years, and I felt like drawing her out. There were dueling interests at heart; that of lending a helping hand, and a self-absorbed curiosity. Had she changed, or was I the enlightened? In any event, when she asked for coffee at 3 p.m., I jumped in with both feet. An hour later I felt a queasy sense of fear in the pit of my stomach, so I called one friend, then another, both allies in recovery. One said, yes, perhaps I could be of help, if that was what she wanted. I was strong enough, he said. The other said, no, I was — still — too consumed with the past to think clearly of the present. The second opinion felt more correct, and it gave me all the more reason to see Mary. There is a part of me that will live dangerously, so I stepped into the coffee shop at 3 p.m. I found a corner table because Mary would be fashionably late. At 3:23 — I timed it almost to the second — Mary walked in with a dangerous air of elegance in her step. She looked just as I remembered her in the best of times, and for a moment, my mind roared. She

148

wore a tight white sweater that gripped her breasts, a pink skirt, panty hose (a fetish of mine) and pink heels. Her smile seemed genuine, as did her kiss on the cheek, as did her medicine breath.

She talked of a new job, a new apartment, new interests and a new male cat to join her female feline. She talked of having grown up and of wanting new relationships, of having missed me and wanting to get back together. The words were filmy. The only clear sense I had were the competing smells of perfume and alcohol. She had to drink to meet me? What's wrong with that? It sickened the senses it was so nauseating. I couldn't help but absorb the aroma and lean back in the booth, feeling weak and disorientated. She had to drink to meet me? What's wrong with that? I didn't want to stay to find out. I finished my coffee — she hadn't ordered — grabbed my coat and slid off the bench.

"Where are you going?" she asked.

I stood to put on my coat, searching for the profound. Finally, I shrugged. "Mary, I just can't do this."

"Do what?" she said, almost pleading. "We'll take it slow. I promise."

I set a couple of singles on the table. "I can't take it ... at all. I gotta go."

I could feel Mary's eyes burn frustration and confusion through my back. I needed fresh air; I needed a walk. To where? Home, only six blocks away, seemed too close and confining. I needed to be aimless with a prayer of revelation. So I went three blocks north, two blocks west ... instinctively, it seemed, to Minit-Market and to the beer cooler. I stared at the mixture of bottles and cans that promised cold taste to the back of the throat, and that I knew would warm the stomach and alter the nerves. I stared until others stepped in front to buy beer, and I began to feel as if I was stalking the beer rather than buying it, so I nervously stepped to the coffee pot for a cup I did not need. I paid and walked two blocks east and

another three blocks north to home, to phone my allies, because I am what I am in cement shoes.

I Dreamt Of Strange Shores
N. Toerrho

I had a dream about you last night
You came in and stood in front of the counter
like anybody else would
and my heart swam, delirious
Then you stepped behind the counter
opened your arms
to me
you said
These Arms Are Made Of Glass
so I looked and being a dream
I discovered that I could see through them
there were
red stained glass lines etched in the shapes
of muscles
blue scratches where your veins should have been
opaque, smoky black
for your tattoo
They all chased each other under the cover
of your Portland State sweatshirt
even though it felt like 90 outside
to me
you said
These Arms Were Made For You
They bent around me, pretty pliable for glass
and they shattered
when you kissed my lips

The world around us went on-
  Yvonne swore at the big machine
    Maria clipped tags off expensive suits
      Carlos worked the presser over the blare of Mexican Folk
Music
        Joanie hung shirts with starched collars to the beat of
          Z89.8 Old Skool R&B
The kiss continued and the glass
of your arms sliced me
in a million places
I thought I might bleed to death
right there on the floor of the Greener Cleaner, 5312 N.
Broadway
This Neighborhood Is Going To Hell Anyway Did You Hear
About That Homicide Last Week Some Poor Girl Slashed To
Death At The Greener Cleaner, 5312 N. Broadway
I expected to die at any minute
with all those cuts tingling and tickling
gushing and leaking for all I knew
Dreams are funny that way thought
my heart kept paddling
furiously, like a sailor grasping at a rope
somewhere between wind and waves
Your lips left mine in a state of chaotic confusion
like coming down off your first high
and innocently craving
more.
You left my body a place of destruction.
I stared down at the pools of blood
around my red converse shoes
and began the long swim
back to shore.

Gut Feeling
Walter Michka

Sweat matted Fred's hair at the temples, formed just above his ears, darkening his blunt sideburns, showing his scalp white beneath. It gathered into a single droplet, welling up, gaining weight and breaking free, slipping down his puffy cheek, around the arch of his jaw, along his neck into his tight shirt collar. This was a good sign— no pain, no gain. He licked his lips, cottonmouth. His blood was pumping. He was feeling the burn. His breathing quickened.

Fred's eyes darted from the cashier, busy gaping at a traveler's check in one hand and an out-of-state license in the other, to the stockboy pushing the Get Wells over making room for the Happy Father's Days, to the cashier again, to the lady with the screaming kid, to the guy frowning into his cellphone.

Fred knew this was his moment; this was it. But what? What, what, what—? The Easter candles looked way too heavy. Wind chimes. Potpourri. Blown glass Snoopys. He backed his way to the rear of the shop keeping tabs on everyone. WHAT! When he bumped into a display of Beanie Babies, he grabbed one. It was a stupid, ugly piece of crap, multi-colored blue and silver with a ridiculous face. He hated Beanie Babies, never bought even one for his kids, even after long business trips, last minute at the airport. He hated their little nametags. The black panther named Midnight. Poseidon, the blue whale. The one Fred took was a baby bird named Dinky, but he didn't know that. He didn't look at its cutesy name when he plucked it off the shelf and palmed it down out of sight, holding it next to his leg. He kept backing down the aisle, everybody stay put, screaming kid: okay, yeah that's it and around the endcap display of marked-down picture frames.

His hair was wet to where it began thinning. His armpits dripped, and the small of his back.

Then he turned around, for just the tiniest moment; he turned his back on the cashier, on cellphone guy, on the store, and shoved the Beanie Baby into his pants. Over his belly, under his thin leather belt, and snug into his white, cotton briefs.

Exhale. Yeah, that's it. Just like that. That's how he liked it.

The cashier suspected nothing, how could she, the little simp, the clueless twit, when Fred came up to the counter and handed her the Best Wishes card to ring up.

"Find everything okay?" she said.

"Yes," was all Fred replied and slid the oversized card toward her across the counter. He had barely looked at it before pulling it out of its slot on the rack. It was big enough for everyone at the office to sign, he noticed that much, and it had some kind of cartoon drawn on the front with some neutered sentiment written in a wacky typeface inside. Good enough for Steve's going away "thing".

Fred pulled out a twenty to pay for the three ninety-five card. The pits of his shirt were sopped. The commercial promising all-day iron-tough complete protection against wetness lied. Yeah, right there. You got it.

"That's five... and five is ten... and ten is twenty," she said with her autopilot smile, totally stupid, completely ignorant of what Fred had in his shorts, "have a good one." He took the change, counted it, made sure to keep the receipt for his petty cash reimbursement.

Half a turn in the revolving door and Fred was golden. Count one. Two. No big hand on his shoulder. Three. No stockboy, "Uh, like, excuse me, sir." Four. Five, and he was— outta there! Home run. Grand slam. A shiver went through his chubby frame and he couldn't catch his breath, he didn't have to, he didn't need air. He crossed the street at the light and headed back to the agency.

Lunchtime on the first decent day of spring had the city's workforce outside, perched on any flat surface, ties flipped over one shoulder, gnawing on bacon burgers half exposed from Wendy's wrappers, or balancing low fat salads on poly-blend laps. Fred moved past the chosen ones, the magic demographic, 18 to 34 year olds basking in the warm glow the entire planet owed them. He walked by them, through them, almost limping, quickstep, slow, quickstep, slow. With each movement of his right leg, every other step, he could feel Dinky, soft and bulgy, in his underwear.

Music played in his head:

The screen door slams. Mary's dress sways. Like a vision, she dances across the porch as the radio plays. Roy Orbison singin' for the lonely. Hey, that's me and I want you only. Don't turn me home again. I just can't face myself alone again.

Nobody in the agency's lobby noticed the lump in Fred's pants. Nobody noticed Fred. He stood anonymously at the elevator bank as a crowd filled in around him. Then Brad walked up. He caught Fred looking across the mob when the far elevator dinged.

"Hey Fred," Brad said automatically and came over. Brad worked for Fred, distantly, about two levels down the flowchart and to the left. They had been in meetings together but Brad never felt he could get Fred's attention, not really. Brad never said the right thing, he figured, never came up with that exact astute insight that shines at evaluation time, the precise little pearl that makes an advertising vet like Fred point his fat ballpoint at you and say you've got something there.

"Got a chance to get outside?" Brad tried. "It's beautiful."

"Yeh—" Fred replied. He was thinking of Dinky in his pants, snuggling up all cozy with his testicles. He shoved his hand in his pocket and, through the lining, held on to its furry beak or a leg or a wing, he couldn't tell. He didn't need the damn thing getting out of his underwear somehow and sliding down his pant leg and onto the floor. Fred forced a straight smile at Brad.

Perfect. Brad blew that one, he didn't know how, but he did, screwed up Weather Talk royal. A near elevator dinged, the doors opened and people pushed into the empty car. Brad and Fred and Dinky got pushed in with them. Fifteen bodies or so standing stiff, completely silent, sucking in each other's lunch breath. Thoughts of last week's layoffs, the packing boxes, hastily vacated offices, kept things nicely introspective and paranoid. They expressed to twenty-three, the doors opened, nobody there, and closed again.

"The umbrella strategy kick-off meeting should be effective," Brad suddenly murmured into Fred's neck. "I've seen some of the PowerPoint presentation and we've got strong numbers to back up our thinking."

"Good. Good." Fred said just as the doors opened at twenty-six and he bolted away toward his office. Brad went the other direction to his cubicle to call his headhunter.

Fred rushed past his secretary Jenny, dropping Steve's going away card on her desk without stopping, made it into his office and slammed the door. He fell back against the wall spent, exhausted, the good kind of tired. He reached deep into his pants and pulled out the Beanie Baby. He didn't look at it; he just shoved it into his bottom desk drawer, the one with the lock, past the Sports Illustrateds, his extra pair of wingtips and bottle of Listerine, safe.

Fred— combed, tucked and composed —opened his door to a crowd around Jenny's desk, laughing and passing Steve's card around to sign.

"I guess we sent out the right man, Fred," Jonathan told him, slapping him on the back. "This card is great, very funny." Jonathan was one level up from Fred on the flowchart and to the right, his boss. While Fred's office was big, near the corner with lots of windows, Jonathan's, next door, was bigger with twice as many windows and views of the city in two directions because it was the corner. Jonathan's rung was the next one on the ladder for Fred.

All the Account Supes, the Account Executives, all the Assistant Account Executives gathered around Jenny's desk instantaneously clicked into the "on" position. Suddenly they thought it was a great card, too, a wonderful card. And Fred was a great and wonderful guy to get such a great and wonderful card. They filled out their going-away blurb to Steve with a little extra flourish and passed the card along with a little more verve. They laughed. There was envy. That Steve, what a lucky stiff he was. Fred took out his fat pen and wrote Best Wishes right under the wacky typeface that said Best Wishes, and signed it.

"I'm late for my two o'clock," he told Jenny. "I'll be in the conference room."

He pushed through his newfound fans and trundled away. Looking down at the carpet, unfocussed, an expression of distant worry forming on his face, Fred shuffled to his meeting. By the time he got there it was already crammed with account people, research people and creative people, way too many for the room. There was one seat left empty, though, the one at the head of the large marble conference table, Fred's seat. After all, this was Fred's meeting.

These thirty or so bodies were assembled in this place for one reason, one purpose — to agree on a campaign, one campaign for a new product launch that needed to be shown to the client in three days. From the very beginning to this very moment, the new product's journey had taken eighteen months. It had been a year and a half of market studies, concepting, focus groups, late night cab rides home, emergency deadlines, package designs, skipped anniversary dinners, research, more focus groups, mock-ups, missed first birthday parties, strategy meeting after strategy meeting and still more focus groups. Millions of dollars had been spent so far and today, right now, this two o'clock was to be the happy ending.

Account people performed their best pointing and frowning. Overhead projectors flashed bullet points of hyphenated business jargon. Fast-paced. Fun-loving. Great-tasting. The strategy, the idea behind the campaign, the one sentence mantra everyone chanted, agency and client alike, displayed high up on the wall. On a huge sheet of foamcore, printed in an aspirational font, it read: LIVE THE FEELING.

Inside Fred's head a baseball game had begun, Cubs versus Braves — Fred on the mic, announcing live — top of the first, two out, man on second, Zambrano was pitching to Escobar. Fred jutted out his chin just a touch and he raised one eyebrow. Over the years he mastered this look of someone who was listening, absorbing, taking it all in, actually grasping what was going on.

Experts from the Research Department displayed their most colorful pie charts of potential target markets, videotaped results of extensive ethnographic field studies and a couple of collages for good measure. High and outside... ball three... count goes to three and two. Zambrano was in a tight spot early in the third. Fred nodded his head, pursed his lips slightly and feverishly scribbled in his leather-bound notebook.

Tattooed creative teams with tongue piercings covered the room with edgy storyboards and moodboards, edgy print ads and website ideas. They played edgy hip-hop CDs way too loudly and flayed their arms. They read edgy scripts in forceful voices. Ramirez lines one to right field... it takes a fair hop to the foul pole. Lee's rounding second, headed for third. This could bring the Cubs to within one run. Fred stroked his cheek and squeezed his lower lip like a chess master trying to save his rook.

Two and a half hours went by and the meeting shifted into phase two: Talking. Everybody got a turn. Observations made. Insights offered up. Remarks, bon mots and caveats galore. There were first blushes, knee-jerk impressions and gut reactions. Target Segments. Consumer Response Quotients. Quantitative Q4 Strategic Brand Repositioning Strategies. Pop flies. Pinch hitters. Extra innings.

By six-thirty, nothing had been left unsaid. Exhausted, the entire mass crammed into the conference room on the twenty-sixth floor fell silent. Now it was Fred's turn. Time for Fred to make his decision. He had been in this business a long time; he knew the quickest way up the foodchain was to keep his neck in where it was safe. He knew that the best decision was one that could be made later, preferably by someone else. But it was Fred's meeting. Time for Fred to say something, out loud.

"Hm," he started. "I can see there's a lot of nice work in the room. I can see that everyone's worked really hard on everything. But..."

The whole place tightened, a collective wince, waiting for the backhand across the face. Fred leafed through his notebook in one direction as if he was actually looking for something and then back the other. "But, I'm not sure we're there yet. I suggest we take all, um, five... six campaigns forward. We've got three days. We take them all to the client and see which ones they like." Soriano's homer in the twelfth gave the Cubs a come-from-behind victory.

When Fred got back to his office things weren't right. The door was open for one thing. He'd closed it when he left, he was sure of it. The cleaning lady had been through, yeah he could tell, she took the trash, but things were rearranged on his desk, too, he just knew it. Jenny had come in, she does that. He went right for the bottom desk drawer, still locked. He took the key from his pocket anyway, unlocked it, rifled through the Listerine, the Speed Stick, the junk, until he found him, Dinky, okay. Ah. Jenny probably came in looking for a letter or a memo, had to be. There's no way she could've gotten into that drawer; she didn't have a key, he didn't think. No. How could she have a key? And, besides, Dinky was under all that stuff; she never would've found it. No. She came in for a memo and left. Yeah, had to be.

He pulled Dinky out into the open fluorescent light of the room.

"What've you got there?" Jonathan said, just a head at Fred's office door. "Ah, Beanie Baby. My kids have a million of those. Can't tell one from the other. Should've bought stock in the company though, huh?"

Fred pushed a smile onto his face and shoved Dinky into his briefcase.

"So, how'd the meeting go?"

"Uh. Good." Fred managed. "Good meeting."

"Good."

"Six campaigns. We're taking them all forward to the client."

"Good."

"They need some work. But I'll get things buttoned up by Thursday."

"Good. Great." And he left. Fred exhaled.

In his Camry twenty minutes later Fred felt protected, crunched around a block of traffic, Dinky in his briefcase on the passenger seat. Fifteen miles an hour then brakelights all the way out of the city. The bozos and the jerks were doing their evening dance, veering and swerving as usual. There was no use yelling at the windshield so he didn't. His jaw tightened, clamping his molars together fast, pulling his cheeks up and crinkling his face into a grimace, his customary nightly cringe.

He checked his cellphone for voicemail then his office extension. The head Creative Director, the other Big Guy from Fred's two o'clock, called with concerns. He had issues. He found a few aspects troublesome. Perhaps they should regroup in the morning and address — fast forward, fast forward, end of message, erase.

He clicked on a classic rock station.

Tell everyone that I am sorry, truly sorry for all of the wrongs I done. I never meant to hurt nobody, no. Lord, I never want to do no wrong. Now I have lied and I have begged and I have cheated and I know my ship won't be comin' in. As I lay me down to take my rest, I see that it's just dust in the wind.

It had been a complete cosmic accident, back in college. Fred was new to the dorm; he had been across campus last year, sophomore year, and came over because a friend needed a roommate. He was trying to do a load of overdue laundry, wandering around the building with a basket and a box of powdered soap. He ended up in the basement craning his neck looking for washing machines. He found, instead, the college radio station. Low wattage, alternative, it smelled of smoke: cigarette and the other kind. It was all of three rooms: a lounge littered with broken couches and chairs, an office with a small desk surrounded by ten thousand vinyl records at least, and the studio for the DJs. Rust-colored carpeting covered the floors, wall to wall, then up the walls covering them, too, and onto the ceiling. Women, braless women, with long, dark hair sat cross-legged on the floor. They were laughing. The men had long hair, too and mutton chop sideburns. There was only one rule at the station: No Textbooks Allowed.

After only a couple of weeks of hanging around Fred got his own shift — Thursday nights, ten to midnight. There was no news, no traffic reports, no commercials — just music, anything Fred wanted to put on the turntables or say into the microphone and send out to whoever was listening, everyone and no one, anything Fred imagined, anything he felt would go together with the last thing he played, wherever the music took him. There was no Play List. It was Todd Rundgren followed by Bolero then Lindsey Buckingham, some NRBQ before Adrian Belew, a poem, Springsteen, The Chipmunks or Tom Waits and on and on and on. It was a two-hour floating bubble in Fred's life, a rift in time where nothing mattered, nothing could touch him. In the daytime Fred studied something stable, something to fall back on, something to make his parents proud, a dream, they told him, won't pay the bills. But his life was Thursday night to Thursday night, the station, the music.

Then one May morning, along with a couple of thousand other sufficiently educated strangers, Fred graduated. His air-check made it to a couple of second-tier stations in smaller markets before steady employment called from the corporate sector; he never got near a mic again.

Twenty-eight years later Fred was pulling into his driveway for the ninety-millionth time. He didn't notice that his house was a perfect cube — exactly as tall as it was wide and deep. It had always been a cube; the real estate agent showed it to him that way, that's how he bought it. But he didn't notice his house anymore, or his neighborhood or that his wife Alice's car wasn't there. He didn't notice the deep crease in his forehead between his eyebrows that never went away.

He shuffled from his cube garage to his cube house, his grimace getting bigger, his face cranking itself inward like reacting to a dull pain. His briefcase, fully loaded with guiltwork and Dinky, dragged his arm down straight, curving his spine. But that wasn't it. It was something else. He fumbled with his keys but the kitchen door was open. The distant ping! boing! whoop! of Todd, Brian, and Nintendo came from the living room. He swung the door wide as the baby sitter, purse and jacket already in hand, grabbed the knob, squeezing past him.

"I'm giving you two weeks notice," she snapped on her way out. "Starting two weeks ago. I quit. Mail me the check. It's been sweet."

Fred's head twisted fast to catch her swishing away. He didn't know what the boys had done to lose another one. And they'd never admit to anything, teenagers never do. Alice would be pissed; he knew that. She'd be on the phone tomorrow making nice, kissing up to another nineteen-year-old.

Suddenly Fred felt a tugging at his briefcase.

"Wha' you b'ing me?" Katie asked. Two and a half year old Katie, the oops baby, excitedly pried at one of the latches. "Huh, Daddy? You b'ing me somt'ing?"

Twisting his head back from the door, Fred looked down and saw Katie with one latch undone.

"Damn it! No!" he gasped and jerked the case up fast, clipping her, accidentally, in the chin. Her teeth knocked together hard and she bit the tip of her tongue. There was a second of silence and bink! boop! from the living room as Katie looked up at her daddy in shock.

Then: "aaaaaaaaaAAAAAAAAAAAHHHHHHHHHHH!"

Fred closed the latch and put the briefcase on the counter out of the way. Then he picked Katie up under the arms as she continued to wail. He held her out away from him like she was contagious.

"Todd! Brian!" he yelled.

After a very long panicked minute, the boys slunk in, their loose pants fftttt, fftttt, fftttting deliberately across the floor.

"aaaaaaaah! aaaaaaaah! AAAAAAAAAHHHHHHHHHH!"

"Whoa," Todd said looking at the blood streaming from Katie's quivering lips. "What's this deal?"

"Gruesome," Brian added with a nodding smile.

Fred handed his leaking daughter to Todd and grabbed the briefcase. "Put some ice on that Brian," he said as he headed out of the kitchen and up the stairs.

"AAAAAAAAAAHHHHHHHHHH!"

The master bedroom door locked tight with a hard click. Katie's shrieking, muffled, slowly died down. It was dark in here, padded, obviously decorated by Alice while Fred stayed out of the way. Layers of frilly curtains, dust ruffles in busy patterns, thick pillows with no discernible function closed in on him like a Laura Ashley coffin. But, still, it was private. As private as he got anymore. Fred plopped his briefcase on the slick comforter and popped the latches. Carefully, deliberately, he lifted the top. Under the folders and stacks of paper Dinky laid squished into a dense, matted wad. With both hands, Fred reached in and affectionately pulled him out into the warm, yellow light of the room.

Fred twisted Dinky's head forward again, stroked the bird's beak straight, fluffed its wings and brushed its multi-colored fur with his fingers to get the flat parts out. He uncrumpled the bird's legs and set it on the bed. Then slowly he kneeled down, lowered himself until he was eye to eye with it. Fred's whole body went soft, his jaw unset. He sighed a deep sigh and his shoulders finally eased down. He closed his eyes, gasped air in, let it out. He opened them again.

Ah, yeah. This was it. This was the thing. It was here, right here. Yeah, right here it was Dinky.

Quickly Fred jumped up and rushed to his closet moving with steely-eyed purpose to the far back, behind the laundry basket under the shoes next to the firebox. Next to the firebox that held his family's indispensable documents, deeds, birth certificates, next to that was Fred's own firebox, the one he bought for his other indispensable things, his keepsakes.

Two turns to the left to twenty-seven, right to five and left again to forty-two. One by one, Fred took out his special souvenirs, his private mementos into the bedroom glow. The holepunch from Staples — he blew the imaginary dust off and set it gingerly next to Dinky on the bed. The Phillips screwdriver from Home Depot, heh, that was a close one. The unopened tin of Altoids, lay it down. The 1986 Newsweek, smooth its cover. The Lion King drinking cup. Each thing more than a thing. The pair of sunglasses. Each thing a day and a time and a place. That football kickoff tee from Sportmart. His refrigerator magnets. Each thing the captive rush of his pulse beating inside him. Vacation goldfish food. It was almost too much. The Easter Bunny snowglobe. The little Kinko's copy counter. He was liquid, warm and thick. Major League III, still in its Blockbuster case. The can of beets. He laid them all out, more and more, just so, arranged them on the bedspread with Dinky, the new arrival, in the center, the place of honor.

Fred's face stretched into a drunken grin; his forehead crease almost gone. He fell back onto his knees soaking in the whole collection, the combined reply to his parents' dream fulfilled, the entire monument against capitalism, his life's work.

Yeah.

Then the bedroom doorknob rattled violently, someone turning it against the lock. Once, twice.

"Fred?" Alice hollered into the doorframe. She knocked, too, rap-rap-rap, to be sure he knew she was serious. "Fred! The door's locked! Are you in there?"

"Um, yeah!" Fred yelled back. "Um, sorry!" He frantically scooped at the things on the bed — glasses and beets and Dinky.

"Why is the door locked?"

"Oh," he replied as innocently as he could. With a long swoop of his arm, he grabbed at more — magnets and magazines and curiously strong mints. "I don't know. I didn't mean to."

"What are you doing in there? What's that noise?"

"I'm— I'm—" he stammered, shoving the last of his memorabilia into the box and into the closet.

When he got to the door and opened it, Alice pushed in, looking around, expecting to find a woman or a Playboy or a barnyard animal. Instead, she found Fred, just Fred, looking confused.

"What in the world—"

"I— I was in the bathroom, going to the bathroom," he stuttered, trying to make it seem plausible. "I— I must've accidentally, you know, by mistake, accidentally locked the door. I'm— I'm—"

Alice just glared at him.

"Sorry."

Jump ahead three months to Interview Room #3, stark and cold; it was old, had been painted one too many times. "Interview" was policespeak for "interrogation". Fred had never been in an interview room before. He had only been in a police station a few times in his life— to pay a parking ticket or report a stolen bike —but always on the other side of the bulletproof glass, the nice side of the buzz-in door, never in one of these rooms. He had seen plenty on TV. This one was somewhere between NYPD Blue and Baretta, closer to Law & Order. There was a simple metal table, three stiff chairs, a filing cabinet and a phone. A mirror on one wall that Fred assumed was two-way and a bulletin board on the other covered with pieces of paper he didn't read. Outside, the station rumbled with the usual people sounds, telephone chirps, the humma-humma of serving and protecting.

Where was Jenny, he wondered, with the bail money? Maybe she couldn't find an ATM. Maybe Jonathan wouldn't let her leave work; he asked too many questions and then refused to let her go. Maybe she couldn't find the place.

Fred sat slumped at the table, numb. He had finished the water the arresting officers had given him. He had torn the Styrofoam cup to shreds and was now, one by one, tearing the shreds to shreds. Arresting officers, Fred thought, had such a Nightly News ring to it.

The arresting officers were just two poor beat cops who got flagged down when the Seven-Eleven manager wouldn't let Fred pay for the Slim Jim he had under his shirt when he left the store, when the manager wouldn't calm down, when the manager wouldn't listen to reason.

"I'm through gettin' ripped off," he yelled at Fred, poking him with a bony finger. "You think you can come in here and take what you want and not pay me?" Then to the cops, "You take him away. You take him to jail!"

The officers didn't handcuff Fred; they did him that favor, even though the manager insisted on it repeatedly. But they led him out into the hot, summer street to the waiting paddy wagon. The growing bunch of lunchtime gawkers pushed in from both sides trying to catch a glimpse of Public Enemy Number 3,427,623. The whole Banana Republic was outside, working on their tans, checkin' each other out, telling their cellphones about some Seven-Eleven dork gettin' busted, dude. The ten-foot walk from the store to the curb was in slo-mo, Fred looking for agency people who might know him. Darkness tunneled up around him from all sides, making everything the faraway dot at the wrong end of a telescope. He suddenly couldn't feel his arms and his legs wouldn't work. His face turned a light shade of gray. The poor cops tried to keep Fred from falling, re-gripping him under the arms but he was too much. They lost hold of him and he thudded to the pavement. The sound turned off inside Fred's head; he couldn't hear the snorting and the laughing. He couldn't hear the cops asking him about his heart, asking him about medic alert bracelets. He winced at the sun then curled slowly into a fetal ball with the Coke cans and the cigarette butts and the dirt.

Then tears. Fred rattled in a shudder of violent sobbing. Hands pushed onto his face, rocking slowly, it all came out. Gushing through him, rushing from him, washing out and away. Every muscle spasmed tight. This wasn't how it went, in his mind. This was all wrong. When the day finally came, this day, when the inevitable happened it was supposed to go differently somehow. This definitely lacked the sweet taste of sublime vindication. He was about to puke.

The cops let the weeping go until Fred came up for air, when he was completely empty. Then they rolled him over like a bug, upright, seated on the asphalt, still whimpering. They peeled his hands from his face and he squinted around, what is this — Tuesday? They dragged him to his feet and over to the paddy wagon. Weak, Fred couldn't make the two steps up into the back of the truck so they hoisted him in. The crowd seemed to like that.

Scooting back, finding his balance on the flat, metal bench, Fred wiped his blue oxford sleeve across his dripping nose. He was better now, he was; he was okay, really. The cops looked at him for a second, not believing, just checking. Then they clanged the door shut and it was black and cool inside.

Fred heard the engine start but his brain kept repeating a song:

White bird in a golden cage on a winter's day in the rain. White bird in a golden cage, alone. The leaves blow 'cross the long, black road to the darkened sky in its rage. But the white bird just sits in her cage, alone. White bird must fly or she will die.

Officer Number One opened the interview room door fast, making Fred jump.

"Someone named Jenny is here," he said as he pulled out a chair and sat.

"Oh thank God," Fred replied, bolting up.

"She's filling out paperwork now," he continued. "Just sit tight. Sit. You gotta sign this," he told Fred, sliding a form through the sea of white specks and handing him his pen. "And we'll have you outta here in ten minutes." Then he left to join Officer Number Two behind the other side of the two-way mirror. From the tiny next-door room, in the dark, they watched Fred through the glass.

"Poor slob," One whispered to Two. "He's got no record."

"That manager's gonna make sure he gets one," Two replied.

Fred shifted in his seat. He looked at the pen One left on the table, gold, a gift pen, commemorating some important event. His breathing quickened and he started to sweat. His eyes darted from the door to the pen, to the mirror, squinting, to his own hand moving, to the door again, to the pen.

"Hey, Tony," said One. "Will you look at this guy?"

"He don't know when to quit."

Fred's hand finished its trip across the table and grabbed the pen, palmed it and pulled it, fast, into his lap. His blood was pumping. He licked his lips; he wished he had that water right now. Then Fred eased the policeman's pen into his front pants pocket. Yeah, that's it. Just like that. That's just how he liked it.

Refrigerator Mom
Rebecca Foust

They called them cold and withholding
"refrigerator mothers," indicted them
with their kids' autism. You did it too,
you soul-less suck of a self-righteous
so-called psychologist, with your

"walks outside" and "talks up in trees"
that never leafed out. You wasted time
sitting mute next to my son's muteness
for two years getting other work done,
explained how my "helicopter-mothering"

was causing the problems, how maybe
I was the one that ought to be medicated.
It was convenient for a time having me
Paxiled; no more second-guessing
the doctor's advice to chill out, no more

nagging about homework, chores,
computer, TV. I learned the art of aloof,
how to sleep while awake, how to
speak softly or not speak at all, how not
to feel desire or desire to weep.

For nearly a year in our house,
a kind of peace reigned, until one day
it cracked and rained pieces
of everything—propellers, coils, struts,
random refrigerator parts.

Show Your Work
Rebecca Foust

My son is not good at emotion,
or doing things
to ease understanding;
does not usually notice
when people are displeased.

In preschool, his peers
absorbed social hierarchies
and nonverbal cues, but
he showed a preference
for algorithms.

In math class he got D's
for not showing his work.
He must have cheated, because
no one can understand
a theorem without proving it,

especially not the teachers
who taught him the discipline
of showing his work;
hours spent sitting with
the slow, wayward pencil

gripped at the odd angle, to lay
down the evidence for what

he'd grasped in a breath. We
told him he'd be glad later,
when the math got too hard

to do in his head. Years later
he told me all that work
was made-up, what he imagined
the rest of us needed to find
the answer

that came to him like a whole,
unbidden horizon moon.
I don't do math, so in my mind
the work showed
goes like this:

(-) small-talking
(-) planning
(-) reviewing your day
(-) worrying about the thousand details
that do not concern this problem
+ look inward
+ get up from your chair
+ walk through the dark house
+ climb each step to the back deck door
+ feel the latch
+ slide the bolt
+ walk into the clarity
and stillness
of the dark night air where

———————————————————————————————
= it is possible to look up and stare
at an infinity of moon.

Homage To Teachers

Rebecca Foust

Ring the bell for Ms. Ruto,
gentle and neutral when she described
him sitting on the first grade rug

facing *this way* while the rest
of the class faced *that way*;
Ring it for Doc, who piled desk

on desk in the room's center
and let the kids climb up to sail their
own Mayflower; who grinned

at our conferences, saying
you've got a live one! Ring
the bell for Ms. Stone, who

debunked the acronym disorders—
ADHD, ODD, OCD—saying *school
is the problem; he needs to be*

*John Muir roaming the fields
with binoculars, and he's trapped
in my class room.*

And ring a last carillon
for Dr. Hart, who took him aside
in high school Chem to confide

that her brain worked exactly like
his brain worked, then made him her TA,
the job coveted by Honors Students

applying to Stanford, but for my son
the reason he went back to school,
why he learned how to set his alarm.

an excerpt from *Making Art*

Lidia Yuknavitch

"The Poet"

The poet is exiting a dream. Her head on her desk, her eyes catching glimpses of things in retinal flashes, the crouch of unwritten words in her fingers.

She sees the world on its side, blurry and colored like waking is. She sees what must be the hairs of her own arm foresting up in front of her. She takes a deep breath, holds it, squints; the ordinary objects of the room keep their secrets for a few seconds longer. She wets her lips with her tongue, which pulls her fully from sleep and activates the nerve-twine and vertebrae of her neck. She muscles up her biceps and *pop*. She's awake.

She is in Prague. Her poet self brought her there. Prague: the way things from history stay alive in some places. Absinthe. Sunflowers. Roads made from stones. She gazes out of the frame of her window, sees the steeple of an 800 year old church, mouths the word *psalm*. Pages of her own work rest under her arms, on the table, in view, urgent. She fingers through them. The sound of the paper is something like petrified wings.

She is in Prague working with a famous poet. Is she? What does that mean? In some older world, time, place it would mean apprenticeship, it would have an order into which art fell, well placed. But it is no other world than this; the now poets position themselves in Eastern Europe, the students of language come to not be in America, everyone is trying to revive the buzz of history. World wars and hidden jars of honey. Night skies filled with sirens or people trying not to let their breathing sound. Sex under cover of bridges. The voice of writers exiled and humming like electricity—oh god damn it quit thinking like a chunk-headed poet. Couldn't all this "energy of history sound" just be the heartbeat of a mange-haired animal in an alley, wounded but not dead?

She stops being nostalgic. She knows she lives in this world, not some other, no matter how old and beautiful European cities are. She's an American poet in Prague. She can afford to be. Capitalist pig.

She looks at the pieces of paper, lines, scribbles, words barely decipherable on some pages. She picks up a half eaten sandwich. She wishes she were in a movie she has seen instead of where she is. No, it is not *where* she is that is the problem. It is *who* she is. Fuck it. She reaches over and pours an ounce of absinthe into a reservoir pontarlier glass. The bulbous bottom swells with wet. Then she lays the flat, silver perforated spoon across the rim and places a single cube of sugar on its face. She next drips ice-cold purified water over the sugar, until the color rises, until the gradual louche—what a great word, *louche*—the clouding, also, dubious, shady, disreputable. God damn great.

She lights a fire in the little room. The heat brings on a dreamy hum of amber light. She drinks. She sits in a 100 year old velvet chair. Her hand moves to her other mouth, beginning the rhythmic throb. Because there is this: she'd rather live in the dreamy blur of everything she knows is dead than face the stark realism of an ordinary hand at the turn of this stupid ass century. What a dull turning it's turning into.

She wants. She makes a decision; tonight she will abandon the esteemed workshops and seek out live porn. It is easy to make a clean exit.

When she makes her way directly into the not American night she is moving partly as her poet self and partly as her id. She passes a man near a bar who says something ludicrous to her. She doesn't speak. Most of the time she's either in her mind, or in her body—thinking or acting. She doesn't talk much. Never has.

When she walks she is aware of three things: the bruise-black effect of the night in the corridors of this city, her feet and their syncopated physicality, and the street itself. The street perhaps most of all, for what is a woman but the street? Not on the outside where her role evolves in direct proportion to sinewy social codes stretching and snapping back like some ridiculous rubber band. On the inside she is a street. On the inside, all women are the street. Its gritty insistence. It's resistance to beauty. It's evering path taking the endless pounding.

Her cunt pounds and her mind swims in an aqua pool.

She drains a flask from the inside coat pocket of a James Dean black leather jacket. She has been given the address to a place—ha—a *louche* place—where a woman might mouth the mouths of other women like serpents devouring each other alive. She is hungry for the poetics of bodies.

What she wants first is to watch. To watch two women not American bring themselves to the brink of animal. The cum, the piss, the shit. Blood and sweat and mouths and salt. Skin reddened or scraped or bleeding or bitten or bruised. *Shoved.*

That violence.

Then she wants to dominate the scene.

She's drunk enough now to think things like the risk is great… for if the scene fails, the writing will.

Of course she finds what she wants, she purchases what she wants, she gives herself exactly what she wants. She gives it and gives it until the having of it becomes the word *mine*, and beyond that even, until her thinking and her physical responses obliterate each other. During the violence of the scene there is a moment when song almost erupts out of her opened mouth, but what you would see, if you were watching, would be as base as you can picture …nothing beautiful about it, not to you, viewer of beauty, and the sounds you would hear in your watching would be gutteral and ugly and wrong.

She sleeps like a baby, heaped there with them on a bed made from women without rules or morals.

She wakes with her face nearly smothered between two swollen and pendulous breasts. Whiter than white.

Polish.

She wakes with the body of a third woman—so black it is blue--spooning her from behind.

Morrocan.

She is between nations and ideologies and mores. The salt and stick of cum between her legs smears across her thighs and ass and on her cheek and shoulder bones. A streak of blood near her mouth, the taste of metal. The scent of the inside out of women is pungent and loud even inside her breathing. She licks her teeth and opens her mouth as if to speak, but she is not speaking.

It is the silence before the line.

Briefly she wants to linger there. Maybe she wants to die there. Then not. She gets out of bed, stumbling like a drunk morning after man. She finds no pen, no pencil, where the fuck is anything? Where the fuck is she? Right. Not her own room. She looks and looks and finds nothing to write with.

A purse on the floor.

She rummages through it.

Women shit. Kohl eyeliners—pen-like.

Paper—nothing nothing nothing. She scans the room in that way that eyes work in the early morning, meaning not much, meaning malfunctioning lens.

Pillowcase.

And thus she begins, the first line already bursting toward rupture in her brain, what other people would call a hangover or the cusp of a migraine. She nearly barfs before she can get it down:

This impression I could ravish us/this blood bodied pang

She gently folds and folds the pillowcase and pockets it into... where is her leather jacket—finds it—pockets the lines on linen into the pocket of her leather jacket. Finds enough clothes to exit, kisses each of the women she will never know nor see probably again in her life (for her this is love, this nomadic revolution, this clean exit from the room of women's bodies to the room of the world), and leaves; her writing has come.

Soon she walks an area of streets made from stones, an ancient area of the city. Passageways become narrow and crooked. The more she walks the more the cadence of walking feet settles her. Her hands are shoved down into the pockets of her jeans enough so that the jeans constrict around her sex. She smiles.

She does and doesn't know where she is going. She was taken there—where she is going—on one of the "excursions" associated with the writing workshops. At the time she glossed her eyes over so that her seeing wouldn't be real. She put everything out of focus and filed it in the folds of gray matter curling inside her skull knowing that she would return, alone, pure, without the chatter of humans. Particularly poet humans. Dumbasses.

Her feet find the place. It is a pile of debris. It is a forested heap of concrete off of the road. No: it is a cemetery. A very old one. Jewish.

The tombstones, once you figure out that they are indeed tombstones, are gray-whitened granite and marble, exactly like stacked and leaning bones. They are lichened-over and covered with dirt and crumbling here and there, in that older than shit way.

This is the thing: there are too many of them for the ground they are on.

At some point in time the upkeep, the keeping the bodies straight, the caretaking of the space itself became secondary to the push of time and events and changes in history and values and politics and ideologies and systems—blood systems and astrological systems and political, geographic, philosophic, theological systems. Linguistic systems.

The thing is this: the tombstones, in all their various sizes and shapes and states are jutting every which way, look like the bad teeth of an old world grandmother.

She is moved by this she almost can't breathe.

What do we call this. What is it. The dead among the living like this—without reverence or malice—simply piling up as compost does organically. She looks and looks. She thinks it may be history itself she is looking at.

She takes a disposable camera out of her leather jacket pocket and snaps several I am not a prize-winning photographer but I sure the hell am a poet photos—all objects and metaphors.

Her mouth waters a little.

What am I looking at.

What do I want.

When she returns to her designated writing workshop room she is tired and she wishes she had a cheese sandwich and a bottle of wine and some chocolate. She takes off her jacket. She sits down at the little desk. She looks out of the window. The lace of the curtains sits stoic and male. She opens the window. The white lace moves more like a woman.

She is fascinated at how ordinary objects can switch genders with such ease and grace. She closes her eyes and breathes deeply. She hears the phone in the hall ring, faintly, far away, not about her. She lights a fat joint and tries to suck into life a cheese sandwich, a bottle of wine, chocolate and all of human imagination.

What do women want.

No, seriously she thinks to herself, smirking, *what do women want.*

She considers the women she knows. Every god damned one of them got pretty much exactly what they told her all along they wanted. Nearly on the nose. And yet every single one of them is miserable. Or if not miserable, chronically disappointed.

Does it mean that a woman getting what she wants is doomed to misery? Does it mean something deeper? Does it mean that women are incapable of contentedness?

Or deeper still, does it mean women were not meant for happiness, fulfillment? That they are desiring creatures unto death, never able to capture the whatever it is, the whatever it is always slightly out of reach, and were it not out of reach, it would be worthless?

Does it mean that the thing they want is back up inside them?

She snorts. She takes another long drag. She looks at the fire licking itself.

Did she make the fire? She aches, warmly. She can imagine her salt taste. She smiles.

What do women want.

Women not her want to be had. Wanted. Chased. Adored. Captured. Then they want the story to stop irrevocably on THEM. Never to move again. They want the having them to be enough. She laughs again and smokes again and drinks and closes her eye... and we think men are the egotists, the narcissists, the womanizers.

Besides what she delivers to other women nearly every night of her life... besides their eyes sucked so far back in their sockets their brains cave besides their heads rocked back their mouths agape their pelvic convulsions gushing salt-wetted pleasure so enormous it threatens the world's tidal cycles... she smiles cock-sure and then refocuses... besides THAT, it is this: it is the relationship between eros and thanatos, and the erotics of that played out on the body of a woman. She smokes the last of the small wrinkled thing in her hand. The room leans, but she's lost in the comfort of her head run now.

For instance.

Lots of women would get a little "pang"—fucking fantastic word: *pang: a sudden twinge, ache, throb, prick, stab* . . . killer word—in their chests if you talked about erotic surrender, especially if you didn't mention the word death—about the euphoric moment when you get to LET GO of a fucking self—orgasm—and here her mind catches a sorrowful truth—many women do not orgasm at all—do they die with some kind of energy all stopped up in them, about to explode, do they supernova? But the women she is thinking of now are the ones who *love* the feeling of surrender. Lots of women would not admit it, or they'd make a joke about it, but underneath the mask of being a woman, inside the rib-house cage of tits and breathless a "pang" would announce to their brains via a series of synaptic firings and sensory perceptions ... a knowing "pang". A "yes," if you will. Unspoken and invisible.

Yes, I love the little death moment. I fucking love it to death. This is how it is that straight women really commit the cliché of *falling in love* with men who can make them cum—poor sods were just giving them what they thought they wanted, a shot of the little death, but what the women end up asking for after that is a stopped man. A man made of stone who will stay forever, endlessly adoring the treasure of her.

Furthermore.

Lots of other women would get the "pang" were one to, not looking any of them in the eye, begin to discuss being taken, ravaged, brought to the point of annihilation, shoved by the shoulders against a wall, thrown ass-up over a table, pushed up against a bathroom stall, pressed to the point of crushing against river rocks or tree bark or wooden stairs or linoleum flooring. The same women who think there is too much violence on television and film.

And: underneath it all is the site of a woman's body, endlessly open and desiring, exactly like language itself.

This last thought—that women inside desire are exactly the space of language—she realizes she is a little exclusive in this thinking. Maybe even nutty. Not that others haven't thought it. A few famous men seemed to have gotten away with a thought like this. And a few key smarty pants women have gotten away with performing it on the page, whereupon they were immediately ghettoized into an "artistic movement" so as not to cause any trouble. There they sit, stored in the BIG HOUSE, never to be let loose for real in the world.

Poor Stein. Poor big, beautiful, manly brute Stein. Doesn't matter. Stein's dead. Her thinking takes one last ride on the topic. Of what women really want.

The "pang" of children.

She is not thinking the simpleton: women want children. She is thinking bearing children gives women something life does not. She is thinking that heterosexual union, the fertilization process, the joining of egg and sperm, is lethal to both. Lethal to both egg and sperm.

Death.

Life.

Women get to embody that, carry it, bear the body of it into the world. Death into life. My god, the violence of what it is women do ... bringing life into the world ... is there a more violent reality? She's got her free hand pretty far up herself now.

She is thinking—and now the "thinking" is dislocated from logic or sense, it drifts, her ideas are free-floating, her tongue thick in her mouth, her eyes closed, her head fallen slightly back, her heart drumming and loud, her orgasm rising, and an idea comes to her, and the idea is this: war is the natural response to a woman's sexuality. The violence of creation and the violence of destruction. She cums.

She takes an enormous breath into her lungs. She blows it back out as if she is blowing out honey bees. Her elbow knocks the small glass from the table to the floor, shattering it beautifully.

Then she hears the phone in the hallway ringing.

Someone has been knocking on her door while she was doing all that.

It is for her.

Feeling weirdly calm, she rises. She goes to the door. She moves through it. She moves into the hallway. She moves toward the little technological contraption. In what seems like slow motion, she lifts the black receiver and speaks into it. It is then that she is told the writer has been hospitalized, that she has stopped eating, speaking, that everyone (everyone who matters in their tiny blue marble of a world together) has gathered there at the hospital, and, wouldn't she, please, *come*?

History and time open up like a mouth, inside of which pulses the small pang of an ordinary woman.

Contributors

Josh Ahrens was first fascinated with travel in the sixth grade, when a cousin sent him a postcard from Tahiti. When he visited New York City, six months after September 11, 2001, writing about traveling and those he met became his ambition and passion. He will be in Israel this summer, to learn from those that our magazines and news networks have little time for. He is also working on his first novel, which will be a compilation of lessons learned out there. Special thanks to Jim Grabill at CCC for helping him put it into words, and also to his wonderful family for encouragement and patience through those lengthy slideshows.

Kate Rose Bast lives in Molalla, Oregon with a pack of dogs and a surly cat. She currently studies poetry with Kate Gray at Clackamas Community College. Kate has studied and written fiction with the Dangerous Writing Community. Her work has most recently been published in *We'Moon 2007*.

Becky Browder is in the MFA Program for Writers at Spalding University. She was a finalist in short story in the William Faulkner Writing Competition and in Glimmer Train's Short Story Competition for New Writers. She won third place and honorable mention for memoir in the Writer's Digest Annual Writing Competition. A piece she co-wrote with her daughter Jenny was short listed in *Fish Publishing's* Very Short Fiction Competition. Becky lives in Alabama with her husband. This is her first published story.

Daniel Buckwalter studied English at the University of Oregon and has worked in journalism for the past 25 years. He is enjoying the chance to break out of journalism's conventions by writing fiction. This is a lot more fun than he ever thought, and he wishes he had delved into it sooner.

Sandra M. Castillo is an amateur genealogist and South Florida resident. Her work has previously appeared in *Puerto del Sol, Nimrod International Journal, Lake Effect, The Florida Review, Eureka Literary Review (ELM)*, and *The Southeast Review*, among others. Her collection, entitled *My Father Sings to My Embarrassment*, was published by White Pine Press.

Dani Clifton is a previously unpublished writer living in the mountains of Oregon. Her works are as-of-yet unrepresented. Find out more about Dani at her website: daniclifton.com

Diane Comer's work has appeared in *The Georgia Review*, *AGNI*, *The Gettysburg Review* and elsewhere. She has received fellowships for creative nonfiction from the National Endowment for the Arts and the Colorado Arts Council. Believing what is good must be given back, she has taught at universities in Sweden, Nebraska, and Idaho. She lives in Christchurch, New Zealand with her husband and two children.

Lois Parker Edstrom authored two nonfiction books for children published in the 1980s. Her poetry appears in the Washington Poetry Association's Anthology, *Tattoos on Cedar* and in various literary journals such as *Arnazella*, *Cascade*, and the *Birmingham Art Journal*. In 2007 she was awarded the Hackney National Literary Award for poetry, third place and 2006 received the Benefactor's Award from the Whidbey Island Writer's Conference. She is a retired nurse who lives on Whidbey Island, Washington. Her contribution here, *The Convention*, won First Prize in the Spirit of Writing Contest sponsored by the Whidbey Island Writer's Association, 2004.

Rebecca Foust is a former activist for students with learning disorders, and is currently a student in Warren Wilson's MFA program. Her book about raising a son with Asperger's Syndrome, *Dark Card*, won the 2007 Robert Phillips Poetry Chapbook Award (Texas Review Press) and a full length manuscript was a finalist in three national book competitions including Poetry's Emily Dickinson First Book Award. Also in 2007, Foust's poetry won two Pushcart nominations and appeared in *Atlanta Review*, *JAMA*, *Margie*, *North American Review*, *Nimrod* and many other reviews.

Gary Glauber is a fiction writer, poet, teacher, and music journalist. He lives in New York. More than thirty of his stories have been published. He currently is seeking publication of separate poetry and short story collections, while threatening to write a long-promised novel.

Carl Graham is a custodian at Clackamas Community College who has been haunting its English Department for the past five years like Jacob Marley's Ghost only with more questions during class.

James Grinwis lives in Florence, MA, and edits *Bateau*, a new journal and chapbook press. He has work in recent issues of *Quick Fiction*, *Quarter After Eight*, *Sou'wester*, *Poetry International*, *Bitter Oleander*, and others.

Kyla Hanington was born in Canada and has lived in a variety of places across the United States and in Europe, making all of her relationships geographical in nature. She currently lives on Vancouver Island with her two children.

Holli Hunt attends school remarkably close to her childhood home yet her range of interests and influences spans continents, millennia, and wildly varied forms of media. Hers is a brain which simultaneously commingles Nabokov and online RPG mythology. Her identity is molded both by interests in Japanese culture, with which she is not genetically related, and by her toddler son, with whom she is. She prefers cats over dogs, Belgians over Budweiser, John Wayne over James Bond, and ATVs over AWDs over WMDs.

Jim Irons teaches English and Humanities at the College of Southern Idaho in Twin Falls. He was the Poet Laureate of Idaho from 2001-2004. As a college student, he carried gasoline in his pocket and ate reality sandwiches for lunch.

Harry Johnson was born in New Jersey and has lived in Virginia, Boston, New York City, and currently Los Angeles. He earned his BA in Creative Writing at Antioch University in 2007. His work has been published in the *Aggregated Press*, *Verse Marauder*, *Flask and Pen*, the *Ink Filled Page* and *Paradigm*.

Rob Lavender is an MFA candidate at Queens University of Charlotte. He works at a psych hospital as a counselor and guides patients through Lala Land. He is their shepherd in fields of madness. His work has appeared or is forthcoming in *Swink*, *Monkeybicycle*, *Descant*, *Wheelhouse Magazine*, *Aura Literary Arts Review*, *Happy*, and *Zone 3*.

Michael Maschio is a novelist living in New York City. He is a native New Yorker and attended Columbia College. His fiction had appeared in *Descant*, *William & Mary Review*, *ItalianAmericana*, *5_Trope*, *Exquisite Corpse* and *Terminus*.

Ron McFarland teaches literature and poetry writing at the University of Idaho. McFarland & Company, Inc. of Jefferson, NC, will release his critical study of recent regional memoir, *The Rockies in First Person*, later this year. Pudding House Press of Columbus, Ohio, has published two of his chapbooks, *Ron McFarland's Greatest Hits, 1976-2002* and *At the Ballpark*, baseball poems, published in 2006.

Alyson Mead is the author of *Wake Up to Your Stories* and the forthcoming *Wake Up to Your Weight Loss* (May

2008). Her fiction, essays and articles have appeared in over thirty publications, and she has received the Columbine Award for Screenwriting, the Roy W. Dean Filmmaking Grant and a Writer's Digest Award. She lives and works in Los Angeles.

Walter Michka has written jokes for Jenny Jones, skits for WLUP radio, commercials for Fruitopia, and short films for Chicago public television. He has a BFA in film from Southern Illinois University. To see more of his work, log onto whoozwally.com.

Rachel Newcomb received a BA in 1995 from Davidson College, an MA from the Writing Seminars at Johns Hopkins University in 1997, and a PhD in cultural anthropology from Princeton University in 2004. Her ethnography, *Singing to So Many Audiences: Gender, Identity, and Social Change in Urban Morocco*, will be published in Fall 2008 by University of Pennsylvania Press. Her fiction and poetry have appeared in journals including *Painted Bride Quarterly*, *Kennesaw Review*, *New Delta Review*, and *Crucible*.

Shelagh Powers is currently working on her MFA in Creative Writing at American University. She also works on *Folio: A Literary Journal at American University*, and *The Messenger*, American's MFA alumni newsletter. She received her Bachelor's degree in English from Fordham University, and hopes to work as both a writer and a teacher after she graduates from American this May. Her works has previously been published in *The Ampersand*. Ms. Powers lives in Washington, D.C.

Sarah Rosenthal is a fourth-year student at SUNY Purchase, majoring in Language & Culture with a specialization in Spanish. She is currently working on a translation of Federico Garcia Lorca's early unedited prose as well as a memoir from which this piece is extracted.

Anne Lesley Selcer's work has recently appeared in the *Northwest Edge III* anthology, *Helen's Cookbook* and in an artist project from the Emily Carr Institute Press based on Nabakov's *Pale Fire*. She has contributed texts to several art catalogues and in 2005 was commissioned to write the text for *Banlieusard*, an image-text book based on the work of two Vancouver, BC artists. Her essays and reviews been published by *The Fillip Review*, *doppelgangermagazine.com* and *Artforum*, and include a forthcoming piece on Lawrence Weiner and language based poetics. She began the *Chroma Reading Series*.

David Shattuck was born and spent most of his life in Texas, where he received an M.A. in Creative Writing from the University of North Texas. He currently lives among the pine trees of Eastern Washington and is an MFA candidate at Eastern Washington University. He enjoys rowing upstream, jumping from heights too high, and biting off more than he can chew.

Avery Slater's work has appeared or is forthcoming in *North American Review*, *CutBank*, *Chelsea*, *Borderlands*, *Permafrost*, *Yemassee*, and many other journals. She holds an M.F.A. from the University of Washington and an M.Phil. in English from the University of Cambridge.

David Starkey directed the creative writing program at Santa Barbara City College and is the author of a textbook, *Poetry Writing: Theme and Variations* (McGraw-Hill, 1999), as well as several collections of poems from small presses, most recently *Starkey's Book of States* (Boson Books, 2007), *Adventures of the Minor Poet* (Artamo Press, 2007), *Ways of Being Dead: New and Selected Poems* (Artamo, 2006), *David Starkey's Greatest Hits* (Pudding House, 2002) and *Fear of Everything*, winner of Palanquin Press's Spring 2000 chapbook contest. In addition, over the past eighteen years he has published more than 400 poems in literary magazines such as *American Scholar*, *Antioch Review*, *Beloit Poetry Journal*, *Cutbank*, *Faultline*, *Greensboro Review*, *The Journal*, *Massachusetts Review*, *Mid-American Review*, *Nebraska Review*, *Notre Dame Review*, *Poet Lore*, *Poetry East*, *South Dakota Review*, *Southern Humanities Review*, *Southern Poetry Review*, *Sycamore Review*, *Texas Review*, and *Wormwood Review*. With Paul Willis, he co-edited *In a Fine Frenzy: Poets Respond to Shakespeare* (Iowa, 2005), and he is the editor of *Living Blue in the Red States* (Nebraska, 2007). *Keywords in Creative Writing*, which he co-authored with the late Wendy Bishop, was published in 2006 by Utah State University Press. In Fall of 2008 Bedford/St. Martin's will publish his introductory textbook, *Creative Writing: Four Genres in Brief*.

N. Toerrho is a resident of like, five different states. She's lived up and down the west coast and all over Chicago, where she currently resides. She coaches middle school track with a fierce whistle and wanders through dead-end jobs that support her slam poetry habit. You can catch her at Goodbye to the

Neon Hand on Saturday nights, or out running somewhere in Chicago. This is her first time being published in a reputable journal, although several pieces have appeared in less notable places.

Lidia Yuknavitch is the author of three collections of short fictions-- *Real to Reel* (FC2, 2002), *Her Other Mouths* (House of Bones Press, 1997) and *Liberty's Excess* (FC2, 2000)-- and a book of criticism, *Allegories of Violence* (Routledge, 2000). Her writing has appeared in *Postmodern Culture*, *Fiction International*, *Another Chicago Magazine*, *Zyzzyva*, *Critical Matrix*, *Other Voices*, and elsewhere, and in the anthologies *Representing Bisexualities* (NYU Press) and *Third Wave Agenda* (University of Minnesota Press). She has been the co-editor of *Northwest Edge: Deviant Fictions* and the editor of *two girls review*. She teaches fiction writing and literature in Oregon.

186

Epiphanies...

www.ingramcontent.com/pod-product-compliance
Lightning Source LLC
Chambersburg PA
CBHW020436180626
46812CB00003B/1260